TANGLED WEBS

By

Andrea Lewsley

Copyright Andrea Lewsley 2016

All rights reserved.

No part of this publication may be copied, produced, stored or transmitted in any form or means without the author's written consent

All characters and events in this book are fictitious. Although 'Invincible' allowed me to use his real wrestling name all events surrounding him are fictitious. However he is afraid of dentists...and needles...and....um...spiders.

Thank you to Alnwick Lodge for allowing me to 'use' their unique B & B – a place well worth a visit

For Catherine Richmond

And

Members of The Byre Writers

Thank you for your positive feedback,
enthusiasm and encouragement

Tangled Webs

CHAPTER ONE

'Exercise, that's what you need,' Katrin prodded Lorna, rather unkindly she thought, in the midriff. 'Come to badminton with us, Lorna, it's fun.'

Lorna's frightened mind skittered painfully through all her other attempts at getting fit. "Fun" was definitely not the first adjective that sprung to mind.

What about the cycling? As she recalled she was to enjoy the beautiful countryside and invigorating fresh air. No-one mentioned skew saddles or bikes with faulty brakes, did they? Oh, she got close to nature alright, head first over the handle bars into a clump of nettles. The nurse in Casualty had never seen someone stung in the face like that before. Let's not even mention saddle sore. The saddle rose up at an awkward angle and the adjustable bit... wasn't. Suffice to say she made cowboys look positively straight legged.

What was the next bright idea? Ice skating, that was it. She was to be the graceful Torvill just waiting for her handsome Dean to sweep her off her feet. Instead it was a spotty teenager who sent her flying, straight off to hospital with a sprained ankle and a huge bruise in the nether regions. She's added the doctor and nurses at the local emergency department to her Christmas card list but has no wish to visit them again soon.

She loathed the Line Dancing phase her dear friends went through, boots and tassels are not her scene. She doesn't like hats of any description and she secretly quite liked the music but not the female singer who screeched the lyrics at the hapless dancers. All whilst a ten-ton cowboy leapt on your toes. Do you see a trend starting to emerge? Why does physical exercise always involve wearing silly clothing?

'What would I have to wear,' Lorna asked suspiciously.

'Shorts and a baggy t-shirt will do.'

Baggy she could live with, it's a very undervalued word she'd always thought. Many an elicit mars bar can be hidden under "baggy". To her it represents cool, comfort and most of all concealment.

The trips to the gym had been a nightmare, why is lycra always in such lurid colours? You are handed a putrid pink thing with odious orange detail, which would barely cover a healthy two-year old, in exchange for a large fistful of money. You are then expected to ooze all your womanly lumps and bumps into it. Well her body doesn't ooze. The equipment would be recognizable only to someone who had studied the Spanish Inquisition in depth. Gyms are always staffed by skinny clones from a distant planet who have survived on a shared lettuce leaf eaten over the last decade.

Lorna eyed Katrin's svelte figure enviously, she didn't know the meaning of the word "diet". She was one of those, sickeningly, tall, naturally slim people. Amy is tiny, like a little doll with everything in proportion.

'Come on, what do you have to lose?' Kat cajoled.

'Only a few pounds,' Amy giggled.

Honestly, she didn't know why she called these two her friends.

'Thank you, ladies but no thanks, never, no, no way, not on your Nellie...'

The next Monday, after work, found her standing, freezing, outside the badminton hall in Dundee, on a bitter November night, wearing comfy baggy shorts and equally baggy t-shirt under a baggy jog suit. Katrin and Amy joined her swinging racquets, a minor detail they forgot to mention. The people were certainly friendly and welcoming. A gorgeous man in decidedly un-baggy shorts came over to greet them.

'Cameron, this is Lorna,' Katrin introduced them.

'Hi,' Lorna squeaked as she gazed into his deep blue eyes.

'Hi Lorna, welcome to the group,' he gestured round the hall.

'Hi,' she squeaked again intensely fascinated by

his white, slightly crooked grin.

'Have you played before?' he asked in his deep melodious voice.

'No,' she squeaked admiring the firm thighs beneath the un-baggy shorts.

'Have you brought a racquet?'

"Was that a dimple?" she thought, "please don't let it be a dimple, I just cannot resist them."

'Um, no,' she squeaked. By this stage she was sure he was being ensnared by her scintillating conversation. He strode over to a box in the corner and after rummaging for a while returned triumphant with a wooden contraption previously owned by the one and only Mrs Noah.

'Come and have a game, I'll partner you and we'll treat you gently.'

He could treat her gently anytime. He handed her

a shuttlecock - see she was learning the technical terms already. Another couple smiled kindly over the net. They held their state-of-the-art graphite, super strong, yet super light racquets at the ready. She raised her heavy wooden one and delved through the mists of her memory to school tennis lessons in the '70's and tossed the shuttlecock into the air with wishful, Martina Narva..Navro... John MacInroe-ish skill. She brought the racquet swishing round and resoundingly hit fresh air. Sue and Bob valiantly hid their smiles behind their racquets but her dear friends Amy and Katrin, fell about in raucous laughter. Did she mention they are unnaturally cruel?

Cameron put his strong arms round her. 'Here, I'll show you how to serve.' There was a rumble to his voice and a tremor in the stomach pressed against her back, which she preferred not to think of as a chuckle. However the tremble in her knees had more to do with his nearness and the delicious breath against her neck.

Although the air did get a sound thrashing on numerous occasions, she did manage to connect with the shuttlecock quite a few times and actually found she was enjoying herself. The evening ended with them all repairing to the local pub where they attempted to undo all the good the exercise had done although as Lorna was driving she had to stay off the hard stuff. Cameron sat next to her and she noticed, for the first time, the vulnerable white line round his wedding ring finger, where the sun hadn't reached. He was either an adulterer on the pull or newly separated. Gazing into those clear blue eyes she hoped and prayed it was the latter. She remembered the sadness she used to feel when her finger too had borne that pale, virgin strip. The sun had soon dispersed it but the emotional scars took much longer. He saw her looking and rubbed it self-consciously.

'My wife and I have divorced recently, very amicable but sad. We're still friends, I can't imagine my life without her in it. Megan has always been my best friend and I think that's the problem. We were flat mates at Uni and found ourselves making up foursomes with friends. We were very close and somehow I guess we stopped looking for other partners. Next thing we moved into our own place and marriage seemed the natural progression. I don't think we were ever properly "in love" and that started to show after a few years. We shouldn't have married just stayed mates. How about you? Husband? Boyfriend?"

Lorna's ex, John, wouldn't be able to spell amicable and friends they would never be. Now was definitely not the time to explain.

'No,' she smiled, 'that position is vacant.'

'Doing interviews yet?'

'All applications, in writing, in triplicate will be considered,' she smiled.

There was a faint trace of a foreign accent to his voice, more colonial than European.

'South Africa,' he explained, 'I come from a town called Benoni, near Johannesburg. It was commonly called "little Scotland" as so many Scots settled there. It's a former gold mining town on the Highveld, instead of your beautiful mountains we have mine dumps. They are quite pretty when the sun catches the gold dust in them though. Charlise Theron, the actress, came from there too but, no, I didn't know her.'

His wife was originally from Dundee and they had moved over here a few years ago. Perhaps there lay the flaw in this perfect man, you'd have to be nuts to leave sunny South Africa for dreich and frozen Scotland.

'Is Cameron a common name in South Africa?'

'No,' he laughed, 'I may be the only one there. I had to spell it out my whole life. My grandmother was from Scotland hence the Scottish name, my surname is Pieters. Now I have to spell that continuously, sometimes I wish I was called John Smith.'

Not John, she thought, she'd had enough of them.

'So what do you do when you're not chasing round a badminton court?'

She hated that question. She always got very silly

and over-dramatic as she tossed her hair and fluttered her eyes seductively and said: "I'm an accountant." Doesn't work, does it? Nothing can make it sound sexy.

He laughed at her doleful expression. 'I get the same reaction every time I tell someone what I do.' He grabbed both her hands in his. 'I'm a dentist.'

Lorna's hands twitched in his. She had never seen a dentist like this. Women must be queuing round the block for their six month check-ups. Even root canal treatment would be a doddle with those gorgeous eyes to gaze into.

'You want to cover your mouth, don't you? Everyone talks to me through their hands and keep popping peppermints. They say the Queen thinks the world smells of paint because everything is redecorated before she visits. Well, my world is peppermint. Occasionally, for a treat, its spearmint. Incidentally, your teeth are perfect. You have a beautiful smile. I'd let go now but your hands feel very nice where they are.'

Her blushing was interrupted by Katrin. People started saying their good-byes. She hadn't realised it was so late, She'd been so engrossed chatting to Cameron she hadn't spoken to anyone else. He walked her to her car, a gentleman too!

'Take care, especially tomorrow.' He smiled at her and was gone.

'What did he mean "tomorrow"? What was so special about that?' she wondered. She drove home in a bit of a dream. She didn't even notice crossing the Tay Bridge, usually her favourite part of the trip. It was a long time since she had met someone so attractive who also seemed kind and funny. She wasn't looking for a man, didn't want one in fact. "Wary" was too mild a word and "scared" a little strong, her feelings about men lay somewhere in the middle. She was used to being single, having no-one to answer to or consider except herself and her daughter and she liked it that way. She had realised it wasn't men as such she was frightened of, it was her own judgement. If she had got it so horribly wrong once how could she trust it again? Her independence was very hard won and it would take a very special guy for her to give it up again.

She pulled up in front of her refuge, a lovely cottage in the country, just outside Cupar in Fife. It was all hers, no-one to tell her what to do, no-one to criticise - if you don't count a teenager. It was completely dark, the sky speckled with stars. Her jolly, elderly neighbor, Mrs MacKay sat knitting beneath a solitary, lit lamp.

'Och, that's you home then. Did you have a good time at the Babington?' Mrs Mac was a lifeline for Lorna, always there with a friendly word of advice, taking in parcels and keeping a watchful eye on Raven. She also kept everyone amused with her mangling of the English language.

'It was great, thanks, Mrs Mac. Lots of exercise and interesting people. I'll just walk you to your door.'

'Nonsense! I can still manage the gap in the fence. There's life in this old frog yet. Goodnight, dear.' She gathered her knitting and slipped through the door.

Lorna tiptoed into her daughter's room. Raven would hit the roof if she knew about her mother's nightly ritual but Lorna couldn't resist. She looked so young and sweet, her black hair spread across the pillow, her lovely fresh skin devoid of the make-up she normally wore. Raven is fourteen and the one thing that Lorna felt had kept her sane. She was born with a full head of jet black hair, her perfect mouth opening and closing just like a tiny nestling. In a very rare moment of poetic fancy John had named her Raven. Just as well she wasn't a boy or she would have been lumbered with Fred after her paternal grandfather. Lorna kissed her gently on the forehead and crept back out.

The next morning she drifted slowly to wakefulness then made a critical error and moved. Her muscles screamed in horror. She dragged herself out of bed and into the kitchen, every part of her ached but particularly the waist and backside. If she had ever thought about her gluteus maximus since long distant biology lessons, it was as a sort of considerate, built- in cushion. Every woman thinks hers is too large but other than peering at it awkwardly in a mirror occasionally Lorna regarded it as just natural padding to make sitting comfortable. How wrong can you be? Hers turned out to be a massive muscle which hadn't been used possibly since she learned to walk. It now shrieked in protest at every movement. She gingerly ate breakfast standing up. No wonder Cameron told her to take care today. She felt a bit better after a hot shower. Raven appeared munching a piece of toast as she got ready for the school bus.

'I'm taking your black jacket today Mum, mine's in the wash,' she informed her.

A few moments later she stalked back into the kitchen.

'Where did you say you were last night?

Badminton wasn't it? Another health kick, supposedly. I didn't hear you come in so you must have been late,' she looked at Lorna suspiciously. 'The groaning and Hunchback of Notre Dame routine was quite convincing but why is your pocket filled with beer mats?'

'What? We went for a drink last night but I certainly did not pinch any beer mats.' Lorna replied.

Raven threw three mats down on the table. On each was written, " Please come for dinner with me on Saturday night" and a phone number. Lorna's heart soared, did a triple somersault and landed back in the wrong place, beating erratically. An application. In triplicate.

'You've pulled,' Raven squealed.

Fortunately the school bus arrived at that moment. Raven fled all streaming hair, mini skirt and gangly legs.

Lorna drifted off to work in a happy haze punctuated by sharp spasms of pain. It was a beautiful day with a hard frost. As she crossed the bridge on her daily commute the sun danced on the waves beneath giving the river it's nickname of The Silvery Tay. This was their busiest month when everyone did the dreaded tax returns. It was a modest Accountancy firm which catered for small companies, usually one-man-bands. There were just four staff. Katrin was receptionist/secretary or slave as she preferred to call it and the rest of them, Paul, Harry and Lorna did everything else. She soon found sitting at the desk made her muscles seize up again so she offered to make the morning coffee.

'What's up with you? You're smiling, no-one in accounts smiles in January it's not natural,' Paul, her boss, growled. He never smiled, whatever the month. Ever.

Not even when he dumped Mike, the mechanic's box on her desk did her happiness dim. Mike's idea of a filing cabinet is an old shoe box filled with grease smeared receipts. Actually it was just what she needed. It was a challenge after the usual pristine books, plus she had an excuse to keep moving around so the old behind didn't stiffen up. She needed a large area to spread out all his bits of paper to try and get it into some kind of chronological order. No matter how many times it was explained to him he could not grasp the concept of double entry bookkeeping. His ledgers would have made more sense in hieroglyphics. She took over the grandly titled boardroom and was able to keep fairly mobile while actually doing some work. Only very occasionally did blue eyes and beer mats distract her. Honest.

Katrin, Amy and Lorna met up for lunch at their regular coffee shop in the Overgate Shopping Centre in Dundee .

'Don't look now, there's the wife,' Amy whispered.

Why do people always say that? You can't NOT look. What is the point in telling you someone is there if you can't look at them?

'Whose wife?' Lorna asked.

'Cameron's,' Amy hissed.

She wouldn't know who Lorna was so she had a good look.She was an attractive woman but looked too self-sufficient to be called pretty, she was what an older generation would have called handsome. Dark brunette hair firmly held in a sleek bob, slim

25

figure, smart business clothes. She strode rather than walked, cutting a wake through the lunch time crowds. The wave of people on the pavement unconsciously parted to let her through as though she was Moses. Everything about her from her clothes and shoes to her hair cried out efficiency, purpose, goal.

'She's a real cow and slave-driver. Not a smidgeon of human emotion. It's just work, work, work. We can't have a laugh or anything. No personal calls or emails. Not even supposed to have a personal life. We call her The Android,' Amy added.

Amy worked at a large leisure and conference centre. Megan was the director of the conference side of the company. Amy and Katrin had been friends since primary school. When Megan had organized a charity fundraiser she demanded that all her staff attend. Amy dragged Katrin along for moral support. Cameron had invited all his badminton friends. Amy and Katrin soon gravitated to them as they didn't feel comfortable with the stuffy corporate types who mainly made up the guests. Theirs was the only table rocked with laughter, earning icy glares from Megan, and by the end of the evening they had promised to join the badminton club.

'Oh shit, she's coming over.' Amy blanched.

Megan ignored Katrin and Lorna. She looked at her watch then glared at Amy.

'Ten minutes.' Megan barked.

'Yes, Megan, I'm aware of that. I'll be back on time,' Amy replied coolly.

As soon as Megan left Amy grabbed her things, swallowed the rest of her coffee and rushed off. Lorna couldn't see Cameron being married to an absolute cow especially as they were still close friends but she did look rather cold and downright scary. People moved unconsciously out of her way on the busy passage. A real career woman of the worst stereotype. Cameron hadn't mentioned children but she couldn't imagine this woman swollen by pregnancy, sticky fingers grasping her immaculate clothes or tripping over toys happily strewn on the floor. She was the opposite of how she had imagined his wife. Lorna bet cellulite didn't dare seek a home in her sleek thighs.

The afternoon sped by and soon Lorna was being choked by exhaust fumes as she waited in the long queue of cars at the Tay Bridge. She spent the time gazing over the rippling water of the river. It was 5 o'clock so the sun had long since set but the twinkling lights of the city flickered on the river.

Water always calmed her, it didn't matter if it's the sea, a loch or river. It is so much grander than us little people and put her problems into perspective. The view from the bridge is spectacular, she loved it when the water sparkled, when it glowered beneath threatening clouds and even in the mist when it blanketed the water and only part of the bridge is visible, making it feel like you were driving into nothingness.

After just twenty minutes she arrived at her home, an old farm cottage built over a hundred years ago with beautiful blond stone. It is surrounded by fields, stretching up hills and down valleys. There were only six cottages, not even a hamlet. The view did her soul good, it made her whole and strong again.

Raven was already in, her homework spread on the dining table and a freshly made cup of tea waiting for her.

"I am so lucky with her, I must have done something right." Lorna thought. So far the teenage years had passed with barely a squabble. Raven still talked to her about everything, her friends, boyfriends and always sat on her bed and told her all about her nights out. Unfortunately she now wanted Lorna to reciprocate.

'Right, tell me all about him. Is he fit? Single? How old is he?'

'Very, sort of and I don't know, about my age. Now can I get in the door at least. I'll start the cooking.'

She slung her bag down and marched into the kitchen. The beer mats still lay on the table.

'I'll help you with the food, now spill. I want to know everything.'

'It was a joke. He's a seemingly nice man I met at the badminton, that's all there is.' But she wasn't getting off that lightly.

'Three, yes, three beer mats say differently.'

'Okay, he's very good-looking, recently divorced and I guess the beermats mean he's asked me out but I don't think I'll go. I'm not ready for that yet.'

'Mum,' Raven rescued the poor lettuce Lorna was mangling, 'it's been four years, it's time you got out there again. You're not really old and not bad looking. You're going to phone him tonight, okay?'

Kids surely know how to boost your ego, don't they? But she was tempted, terribly tempted. There had actually been a couple of dates that Raven didn't know about. She had felt uncomfortable and awkward. They weren't nice enough for her to consider a second date. She also didn't want Raven

31

to meet anyone until she was sure it was going somewhere and none of them had so far. Her daughter had been through enough and she didn't want a stream of men confusing her. Lorna had it drummed into her for years that children from broken homes grow up to be juvenile delinquents. Everything she read on divorce said the same thing. No-one tells you what to do if you have to get out for your own sake and your child's. So she diligently read all the articles and did the opposite. Children always think it is their fault so she told her repeatedly that nothing she had done had caused the break-up and nothing she did would get them back together. She told her practically every day that they both loved her. Even when John was being a total prat.

The reason some of the previous dates hadn't

worked out was partly her fault. She met a guy, fancied the socks off him, went out a few times then as soon as he got close she ran for the hills. Was it worth trying again with Cameron? Her life was on an even keel, on a placid lake - very few ups and downs. Could she go back to the highs of anticipation, that waiting for the phone to ring, the excitement when it did, the disappointment when it didn't? She was getting too old for this, the big four-oh was just round the corner. But he was lovely, gorgeous, with gentle yet mischievous eyes. A persistent little voice nagged "phone him, phone him". Eventually Raven thrust the phone and a beer mat in her hand. So she did.

****

CHAPTER TWO

'Cameron, hi, it's me, Lorna.' A whole squadron of butterflies had full scale war in her stomach.

'Lorna, how lovely to hear from you.'

His voice was melted chocolate wrapped in brown velvet. They agreed to meet at the Piper Dam restaurant on Saturday night at eight. She replaced the phone and it rang again instantly. She answered still with a smile in her voice.

'John,' he said.

No warm chocolately tone this time. Her ex didn't believe in niceties such as "hello" let alone "how are you". Just his name. The butterflies were squashed by a huge lead ball. Emotions seem to come from the stomach not the heart despite what the romantics believe . She began her little litany which she chanted in her head whenever she spoke to him nowadays. Sometimes it drowned out what he was saying but that wasn't necessarily a bad thing.

"He's not yours anymore. It doesn't matter if he's in a bad mood. You're not responsible for his moods. He's not yours anymore…"

'Raven.'

Oh, God, she supposed she should listen.

'I'm not happy…'

"You never are," she thought. "He's not yours anymore. It doesn't matter etc. etc.…."

He wanted to meet up to discuss schoolwork and his access. Lorna had never criticised him to Raven nor explained why they split up, she just said they weren't happy living together anymore. She wanted her daughter to have a relationship with her dad and to make her own mind up. Unfortunately he was starting to treat Raven like he had treated Lorna but she was stronger and wouldn't stand for it. As she got older she wanted to see him less and less.

John was a handsome man, tall with black hair now silvered with grey. He was ten years her senior and she was totally in awe of him when they first met. She was just twenty one and thought she knew everything.

She loved him and was so flattered that this mature, masterful man wanted little old her. Ladies, avoid all men who merit the adjective masterful, it's just a kind way of saying bully. Before she knew where she was the engagement ring was on her finger and the aisle was beckoning. She doesn't even remember saying yes.

Before the flowers had wilted and the wedding cake stored for a future christening, it began. First he started apologising to people. They would sit down to a meal she had spent the whole day preparing. Before anyone had even lifted a spoon he would say:

'Sorry about the food, the wife's not the greatest of cooks. Darling I think the soup is supposed to be drinkable or is this the gravy? Ha! Ha!'

The embarrassed guests would be effusive in their compliments and she would be mortified, not believing anything they said. She would be hurt, confused and would try harder the next time. The comments seemed so innocuous on their own but they added up, relentlessly and slowly, oh so slowly and her self-confidence was destroyed. Nothing she did or said was right. He was condescending and treated her like an idiot. The degree she had earned at university was treated like a piece of paper she'd won on a raffle. There was no affection, no cuddles or hugs. He only touched her when he wanted sex and even then it was perfunctorily.

Then the silences began. If she displeased him he would stop talking to her, sometimes for up to two weeks. Most times she didn't know what she'd done wrong. After the fortnight of silence he would come home from work one day as though nothing had happened and she thought she was losing her mind. He didn't beat her, he didn't come home drunk and he didn't have affairs, he would constantly remind her as though all women should be grateful just for that. She had no value, no worth. She often wondered why he chose her. She was bright and bubbly, full of fun and he destroyed it. But not for good. Looking back she couldn't believe how low her self-esteem had sunk, she was like a different person.

They had agreed that she would give up work when they had children. She lost a baby in a miscarriage - that was her fault too. When Raven came along she was so happy with her lovely girl but then she was at his mercy financially as well. He demanded receipts for every penny she spent. He probably did love Raven in his own remote kind of way. He played and read to her sporadically, when he felt like it. Lorna felt he thought of them as porcelain dolls he owned. They should be happy with his attention when he deigned to give it but should just sit on their shelf as ornaments when he didn't. One day when Raven was about eight she said something innocently and Lorna saw that dreaded look on his face. He walked out and only returned hours later. Raven cried the whole time.

Lorna tried to distract her and told her it was her he was angry with. He stalked back in, ignored them both and went to their bedroom and slammed the door. That was his fatal mistake though. He could hurt Lorna and treat her like dirt but no-one would hurt her child. He had wakened the old Lorna.

Secretly she began going for interviews, finally securing the job with Paul. She scrimped and saved every spare penny she could find. She found her lovely cottage and then they left. She didn't creep out when he was at work. She faced him. Raven was at her friend, Tamaryn's house for a sleep-over. The leaden lump in her stomach nearly dragged her to the ground but she told him. The worm had turned. She packed their stuff and went. She refused to take any money from John, not even for Raven. He puts some into a savings scheme for her.

'You won't last a week without me, you'll come crawling back,' he sneered.

Her personality came back. Slowly she began healing and even laughing again. She started seeing her friends Amy and Katrin, they went on girl's nights out and all their awful get-fit-quick schemes. Kat is a divorcee too although she goes on regular interviews, enjoys them too much Lorna often thought. She's a free spirit, strong, funny and sure of herself. Amy is quieter and sweet-natured. A petite brunette and so pretty her besotted husband, Duncan, denies her nothing.

Lorna informed the school about the separation, still fearful for Raven. At the end of the first term after The Great Escape her teacher informed her Raven was a happy, well-adjusted little girl and her school work had actually improved!! Take that Mr

Know-It-All John Clark.

A grunt on the phone brought her thoughts back to the present. Why should she let him bring her down? Something exciting may or may not be starting and she didn't want any negative thoughts intruding.

'It doesn't suit me to discuss it now.' She put the phone down, no goodbye - just like him. It felt good, it felt bloody fantastic. She phoned Katrin.

'I put the phone down on John.'

'Brilliant, about time.'

'Cameron asked me out on Saturday night and I phoned him and said yes.'

'Even better.'

'But he's so gorgeous. What will he expect? What will I say?'

'Come on Lorna, you're beautiful, sexy,

intelligent and kind. He's the lucky one.'

'Maybe I should have waited. Done some more badminton sessions, lost a bit of weight....'

'Don't be ridiculous. Most women would be jealous of your curves. I am.'

'But you're so tall and slim.'

'And you're short and sexy. Lorna, you can start a conversation in an empty room. You get on with people, you get them. You know, Cameron said he hadn't had so much fun in years that night in the pub. He said you were so easy to talk to and so interesting. Forget all the crap John fed you. He is so miniscule he doesn't count'

'When did you speak to Cameron?'

'He called me and asked for your number as back up in case the beer mats didn't work. . Go out there and have fun. That's an order.' Lorna could hear

Katrin smiling.

Now she would start deciding what she was going to wear on Saturday for the meal with the delectable Cameron. She wasn't twenty one anymore and she was definitely wiser.

On Saturday morning Lorna was dragged into Dundee by her daughter. The entire contents of her wardrobe lay discarded on her bedroom floor, all deemed too boring, too old, too colourless by her own personal Trinny (or Susannah, whichever is the most cruel). She was hauled away from M & S even though Twiggy shops there now. Apparently sexy and smart don't go with comfortable. After much arguing and trying on of clothes in those hideous stark mirrors in changing rooms, they finally made a decision. Lorna strolled out with a bag containing a pair of black trousers in a lovely soft fabric which draped kindly over her hips, a gorgeous burgundy top with light beading round the neck and a new pair of shoes bound to have her crippled before she left the car park. Somehow Raven had four bags of clothing for herself although a pack of her Granny's hankies probably held more material.

That afternoon was the most fun she'd had in a long time, she hadn't had a girlie dressing up day since school. She had a long, scented bath with the obligatory candles while Michael Buble crooned in the background. She slaps the Dulux on every day as she doesn't think it is fair to frighten young children. Raven tends towards the Goth look which Lorna hated to admit suits her black hair and porcelain skin so she was apprehensive when Raven insisted in giving her a make-over. But she turned out to be a talented make-up artist. She brought out the green of her mother's eyes and a glow to her cheeks perfectly complementing the burgundy top. Lorna's hair is a very light, golden brown, she knows this because it says so on the box and she always believes Nice 'n Easy. Raven straightened and tonged it with her weird appliances and it fell soft and shiny to her shoulders. The new clothes made her look slimmer and the shoes added a few inches to her five foot four height. The butterflies danced in her midriff and occasionally escaped to her throat with a giggle. The pain in her muscles had receded to a twinge helped by the long hot bubble bath, the delicate jasmine scent still clung to her skin. She was ready.

Piper Dam nestles high up in the Sidlaw hills above Dundee. There's a golf course, luxury holiday chalets, restaurant and a hide where you can watch the ospreys who nest there every year. It is a beautiful, serene setting. You can watch fishermen cast their flies in the dam, barely rippling the surface of the water. Tonight was magical and Lorna didn't think it was her rose-tinted glasses. A full moon gleamed in the sky and twinkled in the frost underfoot. The air was crisp and clear. Cameron was already sitting in the bar area overlooking the indoor pool. He rose to his feet with a warm, welcoming smile.

'You look lovely,' he echoed the thoughts she had about him. He was smartly dressed in dark trousers and dark blue shirt. A tiny hint of a tummy above the belt area meant he wasn't impossibly perfect but human like the rest of them. They had a drink then were led to their table in the restaurant, which was built entirely of logs or rather great big trees measuring almost twenty inches across. It was still possible to get a whiff of that lovely, fresh wood smell. It was cleverly designed with the log walls giving privacy between the tables and a little alcove furnished with comfy chairs.

The food was delicious and the company even better. Lorna had never felt so relaxed and comfortable with a man before. She told him about Raven.

'I have a daughter coming up for forty, oh no, sorry that's me. I get confused sometimes the way she runs my life! She's fourteen, strong-minded, self-confident, funny and kind. We haven't had too many teenage tantrums yet.'

'She sounds delightful, just like her mother,' Cameron replied. 'Have you always lived in Cupar?'

'I grew up in a tiny fishing village in Fife. We had discos and ceilidhs in the market and would have to clean it afterwards for the fish coming in at 2am. It was free and idyllic, the cities of Dundee and Edinburgh just a bus ride away. Did the usual back-pack tour of Europe. We didn't have gap years back then nor travelled the rest of the world but I'd still like to travel. I've moved around a bit but moved back to Fife after my divorce.'

She left out talk of John - this was a pleasant conversation.

'What about you? It must have been wonderful growing up in Africa and why did you get into dentistry? I don't think I could deal with bad teeth and halitosis.'

'It's not that bad, of course the ones with bad breath and rotten teeth are the ones who don't come often. We have a laugh sometimes too. Yesterday we had a woman in and she couldn't understand why I kept teasing her about being such an enthusiastic patient. After her treatment I explained her appointment was for next week. Today I had a businessman in, barking orders down his mobile until the last minute, if he could have attached his laptop to the ceiling he would have carried on working. I asked him if he would mind putting the protective glasses on and he very seriously, took them from my hand and perched them on my face! My nurse catapulted into the cupboard trying to hide her giggles but I had to keep a straight face as I asked him to wear them himself.'

He drew such a colourful picture of his childhood in South Africa, the sun glinting on the gold mine dumps, the black velvet sky and spectacular sunsets. Jumping from one huge, rock-hard anthill to another, his weight not even breaking the surface. Running through the veldt, fishing in dams and catching snakes and keeping them as pets. Okay, he had her up until the last one.

'You should be in the embassy or a travel agent,' she sighed. 'It sounds so beautiful, I want to pack my bags now.'

'It is a wonderful country, with a cosmopolitan society. I went to school with people from all over the world. If they could just get the crime rate under control, it would probably be paradise. I miss the sun and the wild animals. That sounds daft, as though I had lions and giraffe in my garden but we went to the nature reserves often and a lot of places still have baboons and monkeys running around. I once went on a school trip where we were dumped with just our sleeping bags, alone in the bush.'

'Weren't you terrified?' she gasped.

'There were wardens walking around with guns during the night making sure we were okay although we didn't see them. It was an amazing night, pitch black with sparkling stars, a low moon and baboons barking in the distance. It sounds a bit naff now but it really felt like we were communing with nature, I felt a part of it and totally alone.'

'What on earth made you come here?'

'A combination of things really. Megan wanted to come back, the crime over there plus I'd always wanted to come. Once you're over forty it's impossible to get a job so now seemed the right time. I want to see the rest of the world while I'm fit enough to enjoy it. Scotland is also a breathtakingly beautiful country, the misty hills, imposing mountains and pretty lochs. The green stunned me before the plane landed, everywhere, every shade of green AND your rivers have water in them! I was amazed by the Forth and Tay bridges spanning all that water. Often our rivers are just dried out, sandy beds. I don't even know where the water in our taps come from here. In South Africa you know which dam it is and the state of the water levels at all times in case of drought. The Scottish people are very friendly and chatty even if they're small,' he alluded to her five foot four from his lofty six foot one and squeezed her hand.

'You said your Granny was Scottish. Where did she come from?'

'Aberdeen, I haven't made it up there yet. I must go sometime. She gave me the address so I can see the house she grew up in.'

'So you're part Aberdonian, that could be a problem,' she teased.

'You don't like Aberdonians?' he pretended to bristle.

'Depends. How do you feel about Annie Lennox?'

'This kind of feels like a deal-breaker.'

'Bet your boots on it.'

'I'm afraid I'm not very keen,' he closed one eye and peeped at her nervously from the other.

'Oh, thank goodness. I can't stand her. I don't know what it is, she's the only one that I have to actually switch the radio off when she's on. If you were a huge fan I'd have to confine you to listening in the shed.'

'I think it's the way she mangles and elongates her vowels. Does that mean I'll be seeing you again?' he asked hopefully.

'I think you're forgetting this is an interview, Mr

Pieters. I am the one asking the questions.'

He laughed. 'You're very easy to talk to, Lorna, I've enjoyed our evening. Entertaining and beautiful. A man could get lost in those green eyes.' She finally realised that the restaurant was empty bar them, the evening had flown by. He paid the bill and saw her to her car. All her nerve endings were on high alert and those butterflies did the samba in her stomach in the moment of blissful anticipation as he leant in for that first kiss. Bits of her anatomy she had forgotten she had came suddenly to life whilst the butterflies surfed on warm golden waves. Oh, she liked this man. She felt a second interview was definitely in order.

Raven liked him too when she met him but obviously not in the same way. Over the next month Lorna wondered if she could keep up with him though as he was so energetic. Hills were be climbed not admired from afar, ceilidhs were to be danced and water to be skimmed over in a variety of vessels. The girls had actually been right, exercise could be fun. The best side effect was that she'd toned up, lost a few pounds and was now quite svelte. She hadn't run yet either, didn't even think of it. The weeks flew by and she just felt closer to him. One night he invited her to his home for a meal. He could cook too, what couldn't this man do? After a lovely meal and a couple of glasses of wine they started dancing . A nice slow smoochy number, after a few rounds of the sitting room he held her away from him and smiled his crooked grin. She gave a faint nod and the moment she was dreading and longing for in equal measure was here.

Surprisingly she never once thought of her lumps

and bumps or felt embarrassed, he made her feel beautiful. She was beautiful and felt cherished like never before. Her butterflies soared free.

She was happy. They had started off seeing each other a couple of times a week and all of the weekends. Soon it was almost every night. Raven loved him too. He had the right touch with her, light, witty and spoke to her like an equal. He spent part of Christmas Day with Megan then joined Lorna and Raven for a fun-filled afternoon and evening playing silly games and ending watching old seasonal films snuggled up on the sofa.

'Don't you think it's time you let him stay overnight?' she surprised her mother one day. 'After all it's not like I don't know you're doing it.'

'Raven!'

'Well, you are. It's disgusting but what can I do

57

about it? You could save money on babysitting and give me an increase in my pocket money instead.'

Raven hated being "babysat" but there was no way Lorna was leaving a fourteen year old alone out in the sticks. There hadn't been any crime around here for twenty years but still. Mrs Mac, next door, would pop in every now and then to make sure she was alright. Raven insisted she was fine alone but occasionally she would return to find them playing gin rummy together so maybe she did get lonely sometimes.

'I might have known you would benefit from it somehow,' Lorna laughed. 'But seriously, you don't mind? It's a big step to take. You have to be sure you won't mind seeing him at breakfast.'

'It's cool, Mum. Cameron's okay and as long as you don't slobber all over each other over the cornflakes…'

Lorna asked him as they danced the night at a ceilidh at New Year. The reels had left them breathless and laughing but he managed to say "yes". And so there was a spare toothbrush in the bathroom. Cam only stayed over at the weekends but it was lovely waking up in his arms.

*

The rain clattered from the purple May sky but Cameron kept the small grin of expectation firmly in place. His deep blue eyes twinkled with mischief as he relished the thought of the surprise on Lorna's face. His jeans hugged his trim figure, his long legs well defined from all the hill walking he enjoyed. His navy blue jacket mirrored his eyes and his teeth gleamed as only a dentist's can. He glanced round, smiling now, happy and at peace with his world. His phone rang and he snatched it eagerly from his shirt pocket.

'Hi, Lorna, honey,' his voice was like rich chocolate left in the sun too long. 'Megan? Megan, is that you? What's wrong? I can't make out what you're saying. Megan! Look just hang ten, I'm on my way.'

*

Lorna got home from work and prepared dinner. Raven was staying over at Tamaryn's house. The steaks were sizzling in the pan, the potatoes baking in the oven and a crisp, fresh salad ready to be dressed. She heard him come in the front door. There was no usual cheery greeting.

'Hi honey, I've got your favourite meal cooking, it won't be long. Why don't you open a bottle of…'

she turned as she spoke and saw his face, his white, ghastly -white face.

'Lorna,' he croaked. 'It's Megan, she's ill, terribly ill.'

She moved towards him but he stepped back.

'I have to go back to her, I'm sorry, so sorry but I can't leave her alone. She needs me.'

His anguished words hung in the air between them then crashed to the floor, smashing all her hopes and dreams. She wanted to cry out her need. What would she do without him? She wanted to be selfish, oh so selfish. To hell with everyone, she couldn't lose him she just couldn't. No-one could need him more than her. They moved as one to the table and sat down. They just stared at each other, his lovely eyes were tortured.

'I found her lying on the floor, she couldn't move

and she was crying. I have never seen her cry, never. They don't know what's wrong, she's been for all sorts of tests. But she's just not Megan, you know? You wouldn't leave a dog like that. I can't leave her alone. She's never needed anyone before but she needs me now.'

'What about me?' Lorna wanted to shout, wanted to scream. They held each other then, their arms tight, clutching like drowning men holding onto a buoy.

'We could still see each other,' he said, hopefully. 'I won't be going back as her husband, I'll be staying in the guest room. I promise. I can't lose you, Lorna but I have to help her.'

But she knew they couldn't. She could not reduce what they had, their love, their happiness to scrabbling around , hiding like it was something to be ashamed of, something dirty. She just knew she wouldn't be able to handle it. The saddest thing of all was that if Cameron didn't go back to Megan then he wouldn't be the good, decent man she loved. How is that for irony?

He left then. A huge heavy chunk of concrete crushed her stomach. She doubted those happy butterflies would ever flutter again. Raven came home and she told her briefly that it was over. No, she couldn't go round there and shout at him, nor could she hit/ kick or murder him and no, sadly he wasn't a bastard.

Katrin and Amy rushed round but there wasn't much they could do. Amy confirmed that Megan was on sick leave. They couldn't do the usual slagging him off, consign the swine to hell type of thing. It was bereavement without a body, no funeral, no celebrating his life, no final goodbye. Lorna worked, moved food around the plate and slept like a real baby, not the proverbial one, waking every few hours crying. She read Raven's homework without pretending to understand it like she usually did. She tried to be a good Mum, she missed him too.

A fortnight later her phone rang.

'Lorna, it's me.' That beautiful voice washed over her. 'I can't bear this, I can't bear being without you.'

She started crying softly.

'I've moved back to the house, to the *spare* room. I've rented my flat out. We can still see each other, please Lorna. I love you. I just miss you so much.'

She had missed him every minute of the day too. She grilled him like a rump steak on hot coals. He patiently answered her every question. Her resistance didn't last for long. They resumed their relationship but apart from a polite 'How's Megan' refrained from talking about the situation. He didn't stay over at week-ends any more but did spend the occasional night. It wasn't quite the same as before but it was better than those weeks without him. Raven quizzed him mercilessly but he never dodged her questions. They limped along quite happily but it was not as blissful as it had been before.

Nearly a month later as Lorna scurried through the Overgate shopping centre she saw her, Megan. She looked exactly the same. She still looked fine and capable, her hair and makeup perfect, her clothes immaculate, as she cut her swathe through the lunchtime crowd.

Megan's stride broke when she saw the nun. Memories flooded her mind. Her parents bribing the nuns to take her into the boarding school early.

Holidays spent as the only child in the school with a

bunch of nuns. The loneliness, the prayers, the

whackings with anything to hand be it belt, cane,

ruler, textbook or even brass bell. Still, she wasn't

that little girl anymore, hadn't been for a long time.

She paused as the nun passed then drew a deep

breath. Her hands glided over her neat bob then slid

down her clothes doing the quick check she always

did before entering the office or boardroom.

Everything was in place. All was right with her

world.

Lorna saw Megan hesitate then march onwards.

She stood in shock not wanting to believe what she

was seeing. He lied. He had lied. Had they been

together all along? Had she been part of a proper

affair? Was he just another lying cheating bastard?

She should have let Raven loose on him.

The nauseating grief was gone, replaced with a fireball of anger burning in her stomach. All men are toads, slimy, warty, self-serving toads and she didn't need any of them in her life. She could live without them - in fact she could do better without them.

Lorna dragged the tatty coat of her pride round her shoulders, thrust her head up and banned her eyes from leaking a tear for a man ever again. Of course the girls came round and they slaughtered a few bottles of wine.

She phoned him.

'You're a lying, cheating, slimy, warty, odious toad and I never want to speak to you again.'

'Wh…what? What's happened, darling?' Cameron stuttered.

'I saw her, your wife, looking very fit and

healthy. I don't want to listen to any more of your lies so do not contact me ever again. Lorna ended the call.

'Right, I'll delete him from my phone.'

'But if you do that it'll show up as unknown number and you won't know it's him. Just don't answer,' Amy suggested.

'I can take him off my email list though, then he'll end up in my junk mail,' Lorna said with satisfaction.

'You can "unfriend" him on Facebook,' Raven suggested.

'Great! How do I "untwit" him on Twitter?'

'You can't.' Katrin said sardonically, 'Once a twit, always a twit unless he's a twa..'

'Language!' Lorna cut her off.

'You can "unfollow" him on Twitter, Mum, then

you won't see his posts anymore.' Raven advised.

'Done. I've wiped him out everywhere.'

'There's plenty more fish in the sea,' Katrin said, ever the optimist.

'Yes, but they're all bloody puffer fish,' Lorna replied, 'and I have piscaphobia.'

'I don't think that's a word,' Amy said.

'Well, it should be,' Lorna declared.

She didn't know what to do. She couldn't remember what she did before she met him. She didn't go out for meals, climb hills, swim, scramble over ruined castles and she certainly couldn't go back to badminton. Everywhere she went, everything she did reminded her of him. This was far worse than leaving John. She hadn't loved him anymore, she had despised him. It was liberating to leave him but this loss was crushing her. Never, ever would she love anyone like that again. It would just be Raven and her. They had been happy before and she thought she would reach some kind of contentment in time but she couldn't go through love and loss again. There is only so much strength a person can have.

She worked hard. It helped.

****

CHAPTER THREE

Summer had arrived in her full glory, warm and green, speckled with colourful blooms. Three weeks before the schools broke up for the long holidays Raven was spending the weekend at her best friend's house. She and Tamaryn had met on the first day of primary one and, other than the usual spats, they were still inseparable. Helen, her mum, and Lorna became firm school-gate friends. She and her husband Phil were one of the very few couples who remained friends after Lorna's divorce. She had found that married women fell into four categories: one - who became incredibly smug with the attitude "I've kept my man, you couldn't keep yours"; two - the majority who thought the decree nisi had changed her into a cross between Marilyn Munro and a geisha and would steal their husbands away, these were usually the ones whose husbands she wouldn't want if gift-wrapped on a platinum platter; three - a few who asked how she got the guts to leave and could they have the number of her divorce lawyer and four - the few, the Helens and the Amy's who were true friends.

On the Saturday night she sat snuggled in her dressing gown and fluffy slippers, a huge box of chocolates by her side as she watched Casualty on telly. Charlie Fairhead, the only reliable man in the whole world (and he was fictional), soothed the sick and injured and ran the hospital single handed. Just as cars, trucks and a bus piled into each other strewing bodies all over the motorway, her phone rang.

'Muu..m.' She could barely make the drawn out

word punctuated with sobs.

Lorna stared at the surreal, now silent, TV as her brain desperately tried to remove fact from fiction. The actors' mangled bodies doused in fake blood mocked her from the screen. Okay, Raven was talking, crying yes, but obviously alive.

'What's happened, where are you? Are you all right? I thought you were at the cinema.'

'We are,' she sniffed in her little girl voice, 'but we want to go home. It's so horrible. Parents are horrible.' Then - the cry of children everywhere. 'It's so not fair.' Her voice dissolved into sobs.

'Put Tamaryn on.'

But that was no good either, she was sobbing and snuffling too. Lorna flung a jog suit over her pyjamas and hunted for the car keys. The mother in her still sped through all the awful scenarios that may face her as the car physically sped through the night. As the shock wore off and she convinced herself that they were both alive if not actually well she wondered what she had done wrong this time but then it didn't take much for a parent to 'ruin' a teenager's life. She was delighted to find them in one piece, huddled together and spitefully relieved that this time it wasn't her fault. It transpired that Phil had been offered a great new job in London and the family would have to move with him. She drove them to Tamaryn's home.

'She's not taking it well at all,' Helen confided. 'It is a bad time for her at school with the exams this year and I hate to make her change schools. The two boys are young enough so it won't affect their schooling and they think it's thrilling. James would rather it was Cardiff so he meet Dr Who but I've convinced him that The Doctor usually comes to London. Tamaryn is devastated, she really will miss her friends especially Raven.'

Phil brought through a bottle of wine and three glasses. He suggested that Lorna get a taxi home or she could stay the night. They'd had a few boozy nights the three of them, putting the world to rights in a semi-drunken state. Phil's company was going through a bad patch, all the usual euphemisms were being brought out, down-sizing, more efficient, time management which in effect meant redundancies. He wanted to start his own business and this contract job in London for a year plus his redundancy money would set them up with a tidy sum left over as a backup but they had to leave within the next week.

Somewhere at the bottom of a few bottles of wine and a couple of Irish coffees Lorna found herself suggesting that Tamaryn moved in with them. After all, she'd slurred, according to "Neighbours" the girls must-watch TV program, no kids in Australia lived with their own parents, they all seemed to live with their school teacher, café-owner or Lollipop Lady for all she knew. Before anyone could draw a boozy breath the eavesdropping girls came tumbling in, shrieking in excitement. Suddenly she was the best Mum ever. It was going to be awfully difficult to retract tomorrow with a hangover, looking into two pairs of trusting, ecstatic eyes.

Strangely, the next morning through a brain fug and pounding headache, it did still sound a good idea. Helen's Dad had been in the forces so they had moved all over the world. It sounded exciting to Lorna but Helen always hated being the "new girl", making friends then moving on and losing them again. She was more obsessed than most parents with giving her kids stability, keeping them in as few schools as possible. London was just a few hours away on the express train, the girls could go down together for weekends and they got more than enough school holidays, every few weeks it seemed. So Tammy would see her parents often and they would come up here for visits too.

And so overnight Lorna became a mother of two. It was a great excuse to finally get Raven to clean out her room properly, they had a spare bed and the girls were rarely apart anyway.

Within a week Helen had her house up for rent, removal men booked, excess belongings in storage and a pantechnicon booked for Tamaryn's move to Lorna's house. Actually it took several trips in the car but she was sure she could have filled a huge truck. It is amazing just what a teenage girl thinks of as essential. She'd never seen all Raven's belongings in one place but she guessed it would look similar. The school and doctors surgery were informed that Lorna was now in loco parentis. She was given a sort of joint guardianship order so she could sign legal forms etc. Helen was just a phone call away and of course they would make all the important decisions. Lorna was the one to do the actual signature without the heavy responsibility. It was mainly for permission slips at school but was there if needed for emergencies. It was a scary thought having responsibility for someone else's child but she'd known Tammy all her life.

There were a lot of late nights with much giggling but they soon settled down. The girls got on well and Tammy fitted into their lives as though she'd always been there. Lorna found she had more time to herself rather than less. Only children tend to get more attention, naturally. Other parents could send their kids outside or to their rooms to play together but it felt a bit mean to send Raven off to play alone. She was used to spending most of her time with adults but now she had a companion. They no longer had the spats they had as children, they seemed to have outgrown them. She worried what would happen when the "I hate her, she's not my friend anymore" started but they had a strong and easy friendship. It did Raven no harm to have to share and consider someone else for a change.

The girls unpacked Tamaryn's stuff, redecorated the room with the latest boy band posters and some with rather large, overweight hairy blokes. The girls, it seemed, were into wrestling. Not something she would regard as a sport but it has a huge following or so she's told. She had never thought it was something to interest teenage girls but apparently she have a lot to learn about it.

'It's not a proper sport though is it?'

'Of course it is. They're very fit you know,' Raven replied.

'I thought they were just very fat, different vowel you see,' she quipped.

'No,' Tamaryn said earnestly, 'they just look fat but they're really strong and have lots of muscles.'

'The training is very good, a real work out. I would like to go,' asserted Raven.

'Won't you end up looking like a big, fat hairy man?' Lorna asked.

'Don't be stupid Mum. They do training for girls and you can choose whether you want to be big or just toned.'

Lorna peered closely at one of the posters.

'I know him,' she said, 'at least, I've met him.'

'*You've* met Invincible?' The girls stared at her in awe.

'Mr Invincible?' she laughed. 'He wasn't very invincible when I met him.'

'How? Where? When did you meet him, that's so cool.'

Hah! She was gaining some street cred here. She basked in the rare accolade of being "cool".

'I met him in Cameron's surgery.' The name still gave a twinge of pain. She had barely spoken it aloud since seeing his wife in the street. 'This big burly bloke, must have been about thirty stone, walked in when I was waiting to go to lunch with Cam. I was a bit early and he was the last patient. He came in with a woman who was about four foot nothing and skinny. She barely came up to his waist and was thinner than one of his arms.'

'Was it his wife?' Tamaryn asked.

'No, she was some kind of guru. One of those new-age types. Dressed in the ubiquitous flowing, flowery dress. She had long, pitch black hair, beads galore and mini dream-catchers for earrings. Apparently your Mr Invincible is scared of the dentist.'

'He's not *Mr*, just "Invincible",' Raven asserted.

'He's never been pinned, you know. Not once in his career,' Tamaryn added.

'What does that mean?'

'It's a technical term, Mum. It means he's never been beaten. Never, not once. So he really is invincible.'

'Not quite,' Lorna laughed. 'He came in clinging to this tiny woman. She started swaying about and waving her arms a lot. She wafted her hands above his head then moved them down his body without touching him. When she got to his feet she started shaking them so vigorously I thought she was having a fit. Cleaning his "aura" apparently. Then she began moving all the furniture about in the waiting room, muttering about releasing the energy. She tutted at the pot plants, gave them a wipe with a tissue, spoke to them and put them back in a different place. Next she hauled out a bottle of aromatherapy oils and started spraying them about the room. Unfortunately she forgot to check that Mr Invincible wasn't allergic to them – he was. After much coughing, sneezing and spluttering, his eyes swelled shut as we watched. She had to open the door and swish it back and forwards a few times until the poor man could breathe. He has asthma too.'

Tamaryn began to giggle but Raven was made of sterner stuff.

'You shouldn't laugh at someone over their allergies.'

'I'm not, it's the woman who was ridiculous. He had to use his inhaler and take an anti-histamine. Then things got worse. The receptionist called him through. The next minute Cameron and his nurse joined us. The guru had to feng shui the room and then hypnotize Invincible so Cam and Sally had to leave in case they fell under the influence too. She finally called Cam into his own surgery. Two minutes later he was back out spluttering with laughter. Mr Invincible was sitting in the chair chanting. The woman had rearranged all the furniture so Cam couldn't even see his head let alone work on his mouth. She had also put all the instruments in a cupboard as "sharp things bring bad karma". So Mr Invincible is sitting there with a pretty, flowery shawl shrouding him while humming and chanting. Cam can't get anywhere near him plus he has no instruments to work with and Mr Invincible is totally oblivious. Cam told the guru to shift everything back again.' She laughed and even Raven gave up her loyalty and started giggling too.

'Cameron's nurse happens to be tiny too. She stopped seeing the funny side when she realised that the idiot had taken all the instruments out of their packets. They have to be cleaned in a sonic bath, fired in an autoclave and sealed in clean packets again. It can take the best part of an hour. The guru had not only contaminated the ones left out but all the new ones in the drawer too so there was not one sterile instrument. She'd opened all the packets "to find the pointy bits" and replaced them facing away from Invincible. Sally went mad. It just looked so funny, these two tiny women going at it hammer and tongs whilst this huge man sat calmly, humming and chanting, wrapped in a his flowery shawl.

'What did they do then?' Raven asked.

'Well, the guru admitted it had taken her so long to persuade him to even try going to the dentist that she doubted she'd get him back again. They decided that Sally would do the re-sterilization during her lunch hour, the guru would sit down and shut up whilst Invincible spent a lovely, relaxed hour humming away. Cam and I would go to lunch. Cam promised Sally an hour off plus he would take her to a slap-up lunch another day. It worked though.

86

Invincible had all his teeth seen to and a couple of fillings without a murmur. The guru then woke him up and Sally took his goggles off and gave him his glasses back. Cameron told him to rinse, he took a huge mouthful then spurted it out all over Sally, got up, screamed and ran out the room.

'Oh' the guru said peering at the wall, 'next time I'll deal with his fear of spiders too. Sorry'.

'They had all looked at the minute spider on the wall. Cam said he could certainly move fast for a big man, he was out the office and gone. He told the guru they were welcome back as long as she just stuck to the hypnosis part.'

'I wish we could see him again, Mum, I miss him.'

'Who? Your Mr…okay, just Invincible?'

'You know who I mean.'

'Just forget him Raven. We're all right on our own aren't we? It's now three of us against the world.'

Famous last words.

One evening a few weeks after Tammy had moved in she shyly told Lorna it was that time of the month and she'd run out of tampons.

'Raven, get some tampons out my drawer for Tammy, please.'

Raven came back with an odd look on her face. She held out a box of Lillets which was wrapped up in a large yellow ribbon and tied with an extravagant bow. Lorna started laughing. She had been in the supermarket with Cameron and was a bit shy of buying them in front of him. She tried to whizz up the aisle surreptitiously but he kept following. Periods and lady matters were never discussed in front of John. When she finally admitted what she was trying to buy Cam insisted he was a new man and had often bought them for his wife. He had asked her what brand and size she needed and had gone to get them himself. She still didn't know where he'd found the ribbon but he had presented the gift wrapped box to her as they unpacked the trolley at the till. The cashier had howled with laughter as he presented it to her like a bag from Tiffany's. She tried to tell the girls what was so funny when a distinctly unfunny thought struck her.

"Ooooh shit," she thought.

"Oh, double shit!"

****

CHAPTER FOUR

It was months since that day. Why hadn't she used them? Why hadn't she needed them?

"Oh, triple shit."

'What's wrong Mum?'

'Nothing, I just need to go to the chemist. I..er..forgot something. It just reminded me. Won't be long,' she babbled.

Initially she'd lost weight when Cam had left. She couldn't face food, she had no appetite at all but then she'd started comfort eating so her weight had gone up again. Had it crept up even more? She was no longer sprinting up hills, kicking her heels on the dance floor nor sweating on a badminton court. Of course she would have picked up a bit of weight. She felt her tummy but it didn't feel any different. She rang Katrin from the car.

'Can you come round? I need you and bring Amy. Now."

She raced to the chemist and caught them just before they closed. She bought four tests, well you have to be sure. When she got home Kat's car was outside.

'What's up? You sounded a bit desperate. Amy's on her way. Is this a one bottle of wine or two bottle crisis? I only brought one.'

'Probably six bottles wouldn't be enough.'

Lorna dragged her to her bedroom and pulled out the pregnancy tests.

'Oh. Oh my God, are you pregnant?' she screeched.

'Shut up. I don't know, if I did I wouldn't need the bloody tests would I?'

Amy arrived and came into the bedroom.

'Get in the loo and start peeing,' Katrin instructed while she filled Amy in.

Lorna did the deed then brought the sticks out. They waited what seemed like five years then they all stared as the word "pregnant" appeared in the box.

'Oooooh, shit. Maybe it's a mista....'

Katrin cut Lorna off by holding up the rest of the sticks all saying the same thing.

'What are you lot up to?' Raven burst into the room, dragging Tammy behind her. 'You're acting strange.' She saw her mother staring at the plastic stick and took it from her lifeless hand.

'Oh my God Mum, you're not. You ARE!!' she squealed. 'What about the rules? Never forget the rules, you said. There are three unbreakable rules about sex. You must love him or believe you love him, socks off but always with a condom on. You drummed it into me. The three sacred rules. Love, socks off, condom on. Be a boy scout, you said. Always be prepared, you said. EEwww, you had sex. Everyone will know.'

'I think it's lovely,' Tammy said.

'I'm going to have a brother or sister. Mum, how could you? Everyone will think it's mine. They'll think you're too old to have babies.'

'Raven, I think your Mum's in shock. Make her a cup of tea as she can't have wine. Go on, we'll talk about it later,' Katrin ushered Raven out of the room.

'You can't drink but I definitely need one,' Amy stuttered as she followed Raven out.

'What are you going to do, honey?' Katrin asked.

'I don't know, it won't sink in. it's been three months since Cameron left so I must be three or four months along at least.'

Amy returned with two glasses of wine and a cup of tea with extra sugar for shock.

'What happened to the queen of condoms?' Amy giggled. She was referring to Lorna's one attempt to be a modern woman. She'd met a guy who was quite good-looking. He asked her out and they had a lovely meal. He didn't light all her fires and was only in Scotland for business for six weeks but she fancied him. After a couple of pleasant dates she phoned Amy and Katrin and told them she was going to sleep with him.

'I'm a modern woman," she declared. "Nowadays women are entitled to have a sex life just like a man. It doesn't have to mean anything. Just two consenting adults having some fun together.'

Amy advised against it "You'll just get hurt" she

said.

'No I won't, I don't love him, he's just okay. I know it's temporary, just a fling. I've never had a fling before.'

'Go for it,' Katrin urged. 'Have a bit of fun but don't forget the condoms.'

Lorna had never bought condoms before. She was with John a long while before they had sex, it was one of the things she'd liked about him – he was a gentleman, huh, or so she thought. He always brought the necessary and they married so soon they weren't needed. Katrin insisted that a modern woman who has flings provides her own condoms. Lorna trotted nervously to the chemist but couldn't bring herself to buy any, they knew her too well in there. Next she went to the local supermarket. Just as she reached to grab a packet she heard a familiar voice.

'It's raining cats and frogs out there. What are you after love?'

Katrin grasped a packet of batteries from the next shelf and gave Mrs Mac a lift home. She turned the car round and drove to the garage, put petrol in and saw them at the till. She planned on casually picking a packet up as though it was a last minute decision, something she did all the time, no big deal, cool, calm and collected. There were dozens of different types but she wasn't going to start reading packets or choose extra ribbed or whatever, as long as they did the job she didn't care about the rest. She put out her hand but was shaking so much that she knocked the whole stand over. Packets of condoms scattered all over the counter and floor. She picked them up, the last packet of "extra sensuous" landed at an old lady's feet. Blushing furiously she thrust them into the box, shoved one packet at the cashier and proffered her money. When the smirking cashier handed her the change she dropped it and the car keys on the floor. She didn't bother with the coins, just grabbed the fiver and the keys and dashed out.

The next day Katrin and Amy came round to see how it went.

'He brought some too,' she started laughing, 'a twelve pack!'

'Ooh,' Amy breathed, 'you must have had fun.'

'And …and….' she couldn't talk for laughing.

'What?' Katrin demanded.

'And… there was nothing to put in them.' She was howling by now.

'What do you mean?' Amy asked.

'Let's just say he didn't rise to the occasion.'

'Well, I don't think it's very nice, laughing at him,' Amy said.

'I'm not," Lorna spluttered. 'I'm laughing at myself, trying to be a modern woman, acting like a man. The excruciating embarrassment of buying them then I brought mine out with a carefully practised casual flourish at the same time he brought out his twelve pack. There we were surrounded by loads of the damn things and we didn't even get to use one! Never again. I'll stick to my no men –no sex rule. You were right Amy, I'm not cut out for this casual sex thing.'

They laughed at the memory and Lorna watched Katrin take a gulp of wine as she sipped her awful, syrupy tea.

'Oh God, I got drunk. The night I agreed to take Tammy to live with us, I got horribly drunk,' she whispered.

'You didn't know, anyway it doesn't take a lot to get you drunk so it won't have been that much,' Amy said.

'We'll need to think of your options,' Katrin stated.

'I'm having it, there's no other option. I couldn't ….you know.. I don't judge women who do but I just couldn't. Anyway I always wanted another child, I just didn't think I'd do it on my own.'

'You'll have to tell Cameron.' Amy said.

'Oh no I won't. This is nothing to do with him. It's my baby.'

'Honey, he has the right to know and he will need to support it', Katrin stated firmly.

'No, he gave up all his rights when he went back to her. *IF* he was genuine then it would tear him apart, he would have to choose again and I wouldn't do that to him. If I was just a bit on the side, which it does looks like, then he doesn't deserve to know, doesn't deserve my child. And that's an end to it.'

'She never came back to work again. She's been replaced. Don't get upset, you just made a mistake,' Amy added.

'No, my baby is NOT a mistake, never a mistake. Trusting Cameron, that was a mistake.'

'I didn't mean…'Amy whispered.

'Okay honey, you're still in shock. We'll talk about it later. First thing is to see the doctor and get a scan. But you won't have this baby alone, we'll be with you all the way.'

'Thanks, I don't think I can do it without you. I'd better talk to the girls.'

The girls were absolutely hyper. Raven seemed to

have changed her mind completely and was excited about a baby coming. So it appeared, she was to be a mother of three. Her family was growing in the most unexpected way.

Late that night after Raven landed back on planet earth and the girls had left, she heard someone crying. Worried, she tip-toed into the room to find Raven fast asleep and Tammy sitting with tears running down her cheeks. Lorna took her through to the living room.

'What's wrong, sweetie?' she asked.

'You won't want me here anymore. I'll have to go to Llll..ondon.'

'Do you want to go? Do you want to ring your Mum?'

'I don't want to go but there'll be no room for me with the baby,' she sniffed.

'What? And lose my best babysitter? Of course there's still room for you. The baby will sleep with me for quite a while and then we'll sort another room. You're as welcome here as Raven is and always will be, I look on you as my second daughter and that won't change. I wiped your snotty nose and cleaned your skinned knees when you were little. You'll always be a part of our family. So, no more nonsense, okay?'

Tammy sniffed again and smiled. She did have a point about rooms though. Lorna would have to think about moving in the next year or so.

'You'll stay?'

'Yes!' Tammy smiled.

'Thank goodness. I need you with this baby coming. Raven is sure to drop it or leave it in her cupboard or something.'

Tammy laughed, hugged Lorna and shuffled back to bed.

The only fly in the ointment as usual was John. The older Raven got the less time she wanted to spend with him. Lorna had found her googling "how to divorce a parent" online. She wasn't going to force her to go, most of her reasons for leaving him had been to protect her. He wasn't keen on "babysitting someone else's kid" and Raven wouldn't go without Tammy so goodness knows what he'd make of the baby. They were at a deadlock. If things worsened and Raven refused to see him at all Lorna would have to seek legal advice but in the meantime she would just let it play out.

According to the doctor she was already half way through the second trimester. She hadn't had any nausea and had presumed her weight gain was because she was no longer hoofing it up hills, swimming or playing badminton. She had slouched comfortably back into her old non-energetic life style once Cameron left. Now she had a valid excuse. So far the pregnancy was much easier than when she was expecting Raven. The miscarriage had been devastating and at least now she was over the most risky period although four and a half months didn't give her much time to get used to the idea. If she could just get the midwife to stop calling her a "geriatric" mum she would start to enjoy the experience. Raven was over her outraged-daughter stage and was eagerly looking forward to meeting her new sibling.

Helen had offered to take Tammy back but they were in a happy little routine at home and besides she would need all the babysitters she could get. She didn't think Raven had been nearer a baby than watching "Call the Midwife" through a television screen. Tammy had some experience from when her youngest brother was born. She was adept at disposable nappies and could set up a tank – sorry, pram – in a jiffy. They all enjoyed the perfect excuse for retail therapy and were soon cooing over cute babygros, tiny vests and little dresses.

Katrin came with her to the first scan. Lorna wouldn't let Raven and Tammy take time off school. The scan made it real. It was daunting doing it on her own, without a daddy, but at the same time she wouldn't have the stress and criticism she'd had the last time living with John. She was more mature and more patient. If sixteen year olds could do it surely she would manage. She came home from the hospital clutching the grainy picture of her little kidney bean.

This time the butterflies in her tummy was the fluttering of new life. The girls were knitting.

'It's what you do when you're expecting,' Raven informed her mother solemnly. Her black hair fell in a sheet over her face, her tongue poking out the corner of her mouth in concentration. The knitting was more like crochet with holes throughout and it appeared to have three sleeves but it was the thought that counted.

Tammy and Raven were due to spend the last two weeks of the holiday in London with Helen and Paul. The girls offered to stay but Lorna insisted they go and enjoy themselves. At first it was lonely and too quiet without them but it gave her a breathing space and allowed her to enjoy her pregnancy at last.

Lorna sheepishly informed Paul that she would soon be needing maternity leave.

'Mmm' was the reply. She worried over this until he called her into his office.

'We've been considering expanding for some time. We had been toying with the idea of Perth or going north to Monifieth but I think Fife would work just as well. How would you feel about running an office in Cupar? You could train up new staff who would take over when you go on maternity leave. You could very well work part-time from home for some months too, if it suited.'

Paul was rather a reserved man and was not used to being clutched to his employees' ever-expanding bosom and kissed repeatedly on the cheeks. He kindly took these as assent. Since The Split Lorna had taken to scuttling around in Dundee, making sure she wouldn't bump into Cameron while her treacherous eyes strafed all the men, looking for that

dark hair, those blue eyes and that crooked grin. It
had got worse as her tummy grew. It had never
happened though, perhaps he scuttled too. It would
be a huge relief to work in Cupar, just a five minute
drive away from home, but she would miss seeing
Amy and Katrin every day, sharing gossip and lunch.

Lorna though she wouldn't need much time off,
say the last month then six months part-time working
from home with the baby. She would be able to keep
her hand in, check on the staff and so on.

Paul gave her carte blanche for the new branch.
He found and leased an office down one of the
lovely wynds, a small alley between buildings which
led to a little courtyard housing various businesses.
Towns in Fife are peppered with them, Lorna loved
discovering all the little shops, pubs and restaurants
hidden in them. There was room for a reception area,

two offices, a tiny conference room, a filing-come-storage room and a small kitchen and toilet in the back. He left the decorating and staffing to her. It was great fun. It was the first time she'd been able to deck out an office entirely from scratch and she enjoyed spending Paul's money. She made it efficient but comfortable too. She ordered desks, easy chairs for the clients, computers and office machines. Telephones and broadband was installed. Some of their clients only came to them when they are frantic over a tax bill or the dreaded VAT return, so she didn't want it to be intimidating. Paul said it needed to be inviting, the only invitation Mike the mechanic needed was a strong cup of sweet tea.

Lorna chose a muted golden sand for the walls, a soft gentle green for the carpet and some strategic pot plants which she was assured were hardy. She, rather cleverly she thought, contacted the local gardening club and told them they could provide the pot plants as long as they looked after them. Lorna has a bit of a reputation as a serial killer of plants. Fife seems to have an abundance of artists so she offered to let them display their works of her choice on the office walls on a "sale or return" basis. This meant some business for them and a constantly changing view for the staff. This brought a sense of community to the office and would possibly bring in new clients.

Next came the staff. Oh, boy, it sounded so easy on paper but it is a minefield advertising for jobs. You can't choose sex or age of course but there are so many things you can't mention in these politically correct times. You can't use words like diligent, hard-working or friendly either. Why? Who knows.

Presumably so you don't offend the idle, the workshy or the anti-social.

Paul agreed to sit in on the interviews to give Lorna some confidence but left the final decision to her. The first through the door was a young woman dressed for a night club. Lashings of heavy make-up and false eyelashes with feathers which ended up halfway down her cheeks, a skirt normally worn as a belt and her very low cut top had her breasts spilling out like over-risen breakfast baps. She chewed gum constantly and loudly with her mouth open. She was concerned that using the computers or answering the phones would chip her nails. Lorna was concerned her voice would chip her eardrums.

Joel came next, he was very nervous and still had problems with teenage skin but he was intelligent and funny when he relaxed a bit. He was a possible.

111

A 23 year old applied for the senior position although she hadn't even done an accountancy higher. A very ex-binman (he'd last worked ten years ago) came in, he just wanted her to sign that he had applied for a job so he wouldn't lose his dole money. A 24 year old young man with good qualifications but no experience informed her he'd have her job within six months. A very abrasive and taciturn man had the qualifications and the experience but would not fit the office family she envisioned. Gladys arrived in a flurry, she'd left her bag on the bus and had actually come in at the wrong time, on the wrong day, for the wrong job. She was so lovely despite her absent-mindedness that Lorna ended up hiring her as a cleaner. She had thought they would all muck in and do it themselves but Gladys would be perfect as long as they didn't expect her to take phone messages.

So many people came who deliberately stymied the interview so they would get the coveted signature to show the job centre they were looking for work. It all became quite depressing until finally Maureen breezed through the door. She was in her fifties, had all the qualifications and experience. She was smart and efficient with a wicked sense of humour. Lorna gave her the job on the spot. A quick, joyfully received, call to Joel and her staff was finally complete. She told them all they could never resign as she never wanted to go through that again.

Paul transferred a few local clients over to them and advertised widely. Mike the mechanic decided he would stick with Lorna and travel from Dundee with his mucky receipts so they were soon up and running. It was wonderful being her own boss, she even enjoyed the extra responsibility. Maureen was

so good that she thought she could run things in her

absence with a little help from Paul. Slowly word got

round and they gained a few new clients, mainly

small businesses although they got a contract with

quite a large company through the art club. They

worked well together and formed a tight, friendly

unit. It was fun going to work and she looked

forward to it every day. She missed the daily trip

over the Tay Bridge but it was lovely leaving later in

the morning and getting home earlier.

****

CHAPTER FIVE

Raven was supposed to spend the weekend with her father but she phoned at lunchtime on the Saturday and begged her mum to take her home. Lorna stayed behind the wheel as Raven dashed out of John's house and jumped in the car.

'Does your father know you're leaving?'

'Yes, and I've told him I'm never coming back either.'

'Okay, we'll talk about it when we get home."

That night Tammy was finishing off some homework while Raven got ready for bed. Lorna brushed her long hair admiring the sheen of the almost blue-black colour.

'Am I embarrassing, Mum?' Raven asked in a small voice.

'What?' Lorna demanded.

'Dad says I'm an embarrassment to him because I won't do what he tells me.' There were tears in her innocent blue eyes.

A fury Lorna had never felt before burned inside her, stoking up like a steam train. If she had seen John then she would have torn him limb from limb with her bare hands.

'You could never be an embarrassment to me. Don't you know how proud of you I am? You are growing into a beautiful young woman, you are clever and kind, empathetic and you have a wonderful wit. What does your father want you to do?'

'He says I don't talk properly. I should say 'do not' instead of don't and he doesn't like my clothes or the way I walk or sit.'

'He never liked mine either.' She nudged her.

'He'd only be happy if we were covered head to toe.'

'In thick tweed.'

'Or even better -in winceyette!'

'What's that?' Raven asked.

'It's what old maid's nighties were made of, with a ribbon tie under the chin and long sleeves. Sweetie, I don't know what's wrong with your Dad but it's nothing you have done. He loves you in his way. It's just a kind of odd way.'

She giggled at that.

'He wants to tell me what to do, how to speak and what to think. Everyone should be able to have their own thoughts, shouldn't they?'

'Of course they should. You have to be your own person and I think you're a brilliant person. You shouldn't change as much as a freckle on your knee.

Dad had a very strange upbringing. His mother died when he was young and I think his father was a bit Victorian. I tried to help him but I couldn't. You can't change anyone and neither should you try, nor should you change yourself for anyone. If you can't love them as they are then they're not for you.'

The following day there was a knock at the door. It was John and he looked livid. His eyes ranged down to her belly then flew back up to her face in horror.

'You slut. I'm taking Raven right now. Fetch her.'

'Get off my property. IF Raven ever wants to see you again I will bring her to you. Do not EVER come to my house again or I will get a restraining order. She is not a dog to be ordered around and neither am I. I pity you John, you have a wonderful

118

daughter and you are doing your best to drive her away. Don't make her hate you, you don't realize what you will lose. I will not force her to see you.'

'I'll get my lawyer on to you. I'll get custody.'

'John, there's not a court in the land that would give you custody. Raven is looking for a lawyer herself so she doesn't have to see you anymore. Is that really what you want? In a couple of years she'll be sixteen and then she will cut you out of her life forever. I thought when I left you I could stop you from hurting her but you just can't stop yourself, can you? Just go and don't ever come back.'

Lorna closed the door and leaned against it. She only realized she was holding her breath when she heard his car engine start. She would have to learn a bit about family law. Could they force Raven to see him? She needed to find out.

Her lawyer told her that if Raven stopped seeing her father it would be up to him to take it to court to ensure his visitation rights but that as Raven was fourteen the judge would take her opinion into consideration. She stressed that they would listen to her so Lorna took this as a small comfort. She had to ask whether her pregnancy would have any effect and the lawyer gave her an emphatic "no". The ball was now on John's side of the net. Lorna didn't know if he would go to the length of going to court. He was spiteful enough but if there was any possibility of it going against him he wouldn't want to face the humiliation. She initially left him to protect Raven and couldn't stand by and let him erode her confidence and undermine her so if it was a battle he wanted, so be it. Just as she seemed to get a handle on one problem another one shot up like a bloody weed.

The time seemed to disappear like a mist burnt off by the sun. Her tummy grew and so did her contentment. There was little stress at work, Maureen was a marvel at dealing with awkward clients. It was lovely to see Joel grow into the job as his confidence blossomed. He was a whizz with figures and no job was too little for him. He was a brilliant assistant. Lorna urged him to do a degree but he needed to work. He decided he would work for a couple of years to get experience and then maybe do a degree through the Open University so he could carry on with them. As she grew larger she started working mornings in the office and taking work home in the afternoon. She was going to leave at eight months but she was feeling well despite the backache and decided to work a few weeks more.

Nature, of course, had other plans.

One Sunday morning after a restless sleep Lorna woke bright and early. She dug the girls out of their beds and started tidying the cottage.

'It's still dark Mum, it's the middle of the night!'

Lorna just loaded their arms with their respective stuff and told them to do their room. In no time she had all the beds stripped. She was just starting to remove the covers from the sofa when Raven stopped her.

'Mum,' she asked hesitantly, 'do you think you might be nesting?'

'Nonsense,' Lorna replied. 'I'm just tired of tripping over all your junk. Can't I want a neat, clean home without you delving into pregnancy books?'

She hauled another pile of washing to the machine when a flood of water gushed on the floor.

For a moment she was puzzled. If the machine
hadn't finished the spin cycle the door shouldn't
have opened so where did the water come from?.

'Oh my God, Mum. Yuck!' Raven screamed.

'Lorna looked down in a daze.

Tamaryn appeared at the door with Lorna's
hospital suitcase in one hand and the telephone book
in the other. Raven panicked completely, grabbed the
suitcase and ran round the house. At least Tammy
had her wits about her because Lorna's had gone on
holiday. Tammy made her a cup of tea which she
drank gratefully, with her feet up. Tammy phoned
Kat and the midwife, then started ringing everyone
in the book. Okay, maybe she wasn't that calm.
Lorna stopped her before she reached the dentist and
hairdresser. Her darling daughter meanwhile started
prodding her painfully in the back, her idea of

massage, whilst texting her friends. Kat arrived and brought an aura of calm to the proceedings.

'This is it, sweetheart. We're finally going to meet Himher.'

They all beamed at each other until the first painful contraction hit. Amy arrived bearing scented candles and an i-pod of serene music. That time at home before dashing to the hospital was beautiful, it was a rare sunny day and the frost glittered underfoot like diamonds. Kat broke every speed limit on their way in while Amy wafted the candles which were starting to make Lorna feel nauseous. She also wasn't sure how safe it was having lit candles in a car while The Stig whizzed round corners but they arrived intact. They were soon whisked off to Maternity and Lorna was clad in a designer backless gown courtesy of the NHS.

Her dearest friends and her two daughters cuddled her and smothered her with love, determined to fill the daddy-sized hole in the day. Braeden Pieters Robson, the most handsome boy on earth, pushed his way into the big, wide world at two minutes to midnight. Kate and Amy held her hands throughout. It had been agreed that Raven and Tammy would wait outside, she didn't want to frighten them for when their time came as Lorna believed that fear makes the first labour so much worse. She did get complaints from Raven that she wasn't fast enough as the mother of five in the next room "just popped hers out and went home". She skipped off again before the swear words reached her.

Braeden was a sweet, happy baby. Being a "geriatric" mum with more patience and self-confidence helped. Lorna still remembered how quickly Raven shot up so enjoyed him more. She even loved the night feeds, it felt like him and her alone in the world, theirs the only light breaking the night sky. The girls were besotted which helped her catch up on some sleep during the day, another plus for older mums. This year Mrs Mac and Katrin joined them for Christmas. There was an avalanche of toys and clothes for Braeden who slept through it all. At four weeks old he was just interested in feeding times. They settled happily into a routine, their strange little family. Of course there were pangs, she still missed his dad, missed having a special someone to share him with, missed what they had. But life isn't perfect, is it?

Lorna was officially on maternity leave but phoned and checked in with Maureen regularly. On one hand she was pleased with her talent scouting talents but on the other she was just a little bit miffed

that the office was running so smoothly without her.

****

CHAPTER SIX

When Braeden was about two months old Lorna

left him with the girls. Mrs MacKay was on hovering

duty. Lorna drove into Dundee. She had some urgent

business with the bank then popped to the Overgate

for some shopping. It was a filthy January day, cold

and rain drizzling constantly. It had been dark and

dismal all day. There was a lazy wind, one too idle to

go round you but went straight through. Everyone

was huddled down, heads buried in necks beneath

umbrellas or hoods but the rain seeped into every

chink in your clothing. Lorna came out the door to

the pedestrian area, she raised her brolly watching

the crowds scurrying past like ants. As she paused in

the doorway she saw someone sitting at the feet of

Minnie the Minx, a statue of one of Dundee's

favourite comic characters. Desperate Dan gleamed in the rain nearby. This person stood out as he or she sat, head on their shoulder just letting the rain drench them. She went to join the stream of pedestrians but thought it really odd that anyone could just sit in the freezing rain like that, it didn't feel right. Perhaps it was a homeless person. She walked over and realised it was a woman.

'Are you okay?' Lorna asked.

She just sat there.

'N..n...o,' she slurred. The rain and perhaps tears slid down her cheeks.

'Are you ill? Do you need an ambulance?' Lorna asked.

'Ye....no, no. Home. Bed.'

She sounded drunk but didn't look nor smell drunk. Lorna bent to take her arm then recoiled in shock. It was Megan, Cameron's wife. Under the sodden hair, her face was greenish/white with huge black rings around her eyes. The woman looked close to death.

'I think I should get you to hospital,' Lorna said.

'P..p..please help. Home.'

Lorna helped her up. She managed to stutter "dizzy" so she walked slowly, stopping when Megan did. It was painstaking. Finally Lorna got her to the car and wrapped her up in the travel blanket she keeps in the boot.

'Are you sure you wouldn't be better going to the hospital,' Lorna begged.

'Need warm, bed, sleep. Got M.E.'

Lorna hadn't a clue what the latter meant. She knew where they lived, Cameron had pointed it out one day and Megan was too ill to query how she

knew the way without her directions. She was
petrified he would be there at the same time as
hoping there would be someone else who would
know what to do. She got her into the empty house,
filled the bath with warm water, put the heating and
the kettle on. It felt weird to be making herself at
home in someone else's house, doubly so as it was
his house. Fortunately there was an electric bath seat
so she didn't have to lift her. Megan was icy to the
touch and her lips tinged with blue. Lorna let her
soak in the warm water while she urged her to drink
the hot tea she had made. Megan slowly warmed up,
her colour improving slightly. She got her out, dried,
dressed in a warm nightie and into bed. It seemed
like she was in another world and barely seemed to
notice Lorna was there. After another cup of tea,
Lorna tucked her up with two hot water bottles as

she could barely keep her eyes open. She refused Lorna's offer to phone someone, luckily for her, and was asleep before she closed the bedroom door. She felt guilty leaving her there but there didn't seem to be anything else she could do for her and definitely didn't want to be there when Cameron got home.

She left with a lot to think about. She didn't know what M.E. was. She'd heard of MS but this woman was obviously seriously ill. When she got home she googled M.E., it had a long unpronounceable name, Myalgic Encephalomyelitis, and was also known as Chronic Fatigue Syndrome. Apparently it's a neurological illness probably auto-immune, with constant flu-like symptoms and pain, crippling fatigue and dozens of other symptoms. Many people had had it for decades and some were completely house or bed bound. It didn't sound pleasant at all.

After Lorna moved offices Kate and Amy decided to make Wednesdays girls' night. They came straight from work to Lorna's every week with a take-away meal and the five of them would eat, gossip and giggle the night away. Tammy and Raven enjoyed it as much as the older women did. They did each other's hair and nails. Raven particularly enjoyed some of the stories about her mother that Kat or Amy let slip. It was good for the girls too, amazing how they confided in the adults and told them about their world in the relaxed atmosphere. It brought them all closer together. That night they had plenty to talk about.

'So she really is ill then?' Kat asked.

'She never came back to work,' Amy said. 'Sorry, I didn't know whether to mention it to you before or not.'

'I've never seen anyone look so bad outside a hospital or morgue. I still think maybe I should have called an ambulance. She couldn't even talk and we had to stop every other step for her to rest. Her eyes were half closed and sort of dull, like there was no life behind them. She barely knew what was going on.'

'Maybe you should have phoned him,' Katrin added.

'Oh, don't, I feel guilty enough. I did offer but thankfully she said "no", I didn't want to face him. She probably slept until he got home, it was only a couple of hours.'

'You did what you could, she's warm and safe at home, isn't she? Everyone else just walked on by, ignoring her. Don't beat yourself up,' said Amy, always the kind one.

'You do realise this probably means he is a good guy after all, don't you?' asked Kat. 'I knew he was nuts about you.'

But in the end nothing had changed. Cameron would still stay with his wife, Lorna would still be alone. She was tired of speculating whether he was a good guy or not. It didn't really matter which he was. Megan was ill, he needed to be with her. Adding the baby to the equation would only make things more difficult. She stuck to her decision not to tell him.

She couldn't get Megan out of her mind though.

The next day she found herself driving back to their house. She checked that Cameron's car was gone but still sat there for a while. There was no movement from the house and the curtains were closed. She didn't know what to do but couldn't leave until she knew Megan was okay. Lorna knocked on the door., As she was about to leave she heard a shuffling sound then the door opened. She looked slightly better than yesterday but was quite clearly very ill.

'Hello, I'm Lau..rinda,' Lorna gabbled.

"What did I do that for? Why the hell did I change my name?" Lorna thought.

'I wanted to see that you were all right. I brought you home yesterday. I still don't know if I did the right thing.'

'Oh it was you. Thank you, Lorinda, unusual name. Come in but you can't stay long.' Megan said.

'No, it's okay. I don't want to bother you. I just wanted to make sure…'

'Please I insist. I need a cup of tea and can barely stand. You can make it. I'm still feeling rough so can't talk much.'

So once again Lorna entered his home without his knowledge. It was a beautiful house, perfectly tidy, a bit too much like a show house for her tastes. His flat had been more comfortable, more cosy, with his personality impressed on it. She couldn't imagine her brood let loose on a place like this. Megan walked very slowly, one had on the wall as she inched along.

'Come into the kitchen and put the kettle on.'

She was as abrupt and terse as Amy had described, Lorna thought.

'How are you today? You had me really worried yesterday.'

'Ah, the infamous dying swan act, as I call it. Sorry. I got an earful from my husband but he doesn't understand. I'm dizzy every time I stand up but sometimes it gets so bad I can't move at all. I never know when it's going to happen there's no warning and it can come on very suddenly. What am I supposed to do? Give up and take to my bed for the rest of my life? Believe me there are plenty of people with M.E. who can't get out of bed and they would give anything to be able to go out. I would go stark, staring crazy stuck in the house, I don't know how they bear it. My husband says I'm too independent but I always have been, I've had to be, I don't see that changing soon.'

'You looked dreadful yesterday and could have caught pneumonia, perhaps you should have someone with you.'

'Oh don't you start, doctors, nurses, the Council all tell me to ask for help. And who would these mythical creatures be? The fairies? The brownies? I have no family and my husband is my only friend and he works all day to support us and does

138

everything in the house at night including looking after me.' She snapped.

"Oops. I seem to have touched a sore point," Lorna thought.

'Sorry. I shouldn't take it out on my rescuer, if it wasn't for you I'd still be sitting there. It's just so hard. I've lost everything that makes me <u>me</u> and yet I'm still here. I can't work, I can't support myself for the first time in my adult life. I can barely walk the length of myself. I don't want to be this pathetic person. I want to be the Megan who can run a conference for two hundred people without blinking, the Megan who wins the downhill slalom race in Switzerland every year, the Megan who can dance. Not this one. I woke up one morning with swollen glands and that was the end of my life as I knew it. Just like that. Now I'm as weak as a new born. I certainly cry as much as a baby. Do you know I've never cried before? I've always been strong, fiercely independent and a problem-solver. What kind of stupid illness has tearfulness as a symptom? Now I sob through adverts, it's usually dancing that sets me off, I used to love dancing.'

Lorna immediately thought of that first time, dancing in Cameron's arms. At least you've still got him, she thought sullenly, then immediately felt guilty. She thought of her life, her beautiful kids, her friends who would never let her go through a single experience alone, her lovely cottage filled with love, her job, her good health even her Mrs Mac with her mangled proverbs for every occasion..

'It must be so hard,' she said. 'Is there nothing they can do?'

'There's no treatment or cure. They try to treat the

symptoms with little success, basically you are exhausted and in pain all the time with the attention span of a gnat – a dead one. God, now I'm droning on probably boring you rigid. I'm sorry. I've never done this before either.'

'Done what before?'

'This caring sharing crap. There's something about you. I've never spoken to anyone like this before. You have terrible eyes, you know.

What? Lorna's eyes were her best feature, she'd always thought. People commented on her lovely green eyes all the time. Cameron loved them but she could hardly say that in her defence.

'They look at you and say: Tell me the truth. They're kind eyes,' she said.

Oh God, now she was bonding with his WIFE! She had her eye on the clock, she couldn't leave

Braeden with Mrs MacKay for too long and the girls were due home soon. Megan was flagging too.

'You're starting to look very tired again. I think I'd better go.' Lorna finished her tea.

'Yes, I am getting tired. You see this is just about what I can cope with, having a cuppa with someone. How do I make friends close enough that I can say "come for a cuppa, now push off I've had enough". Would you... ? No, I don't suppose you'd come again, Lorinda. I promise I don't moan all the time.'

"Not likely," she thought, as her treacherous mouth said, 'Of course I will, that would be lovely.'

What? What was she saying? This was madness but she felt sorry for her. She was prickly and abrasive but she'd been honest. Lorna was curious about her, what made her tick. "I actually like her", she thought. What if Cameron found out though, with her silly fake name he'd think she was some mad stalker.

Lorna tried not to go back but she felt guilty, maybe Megan really didn't have anyone but Cameron and it must be so lonely while he was at work. She called in for a few minutes when she could especially when she knew he was away on one of his dental conferences. She would take her a casserole she could heat for herself later or pick up some shopping for her.

'Milk, bread, toothpaste, bacon and peroxide?' Lorna asked.

'Ha! I thought I might as well be a dizzy blonde!'

Old Android had a sense of humour after all. Once you got past the prickly defences she was intelligent and funny. Lorna walked in one day and her just sitting there but had a twinkle in her eye.

143

Lorna sat and looked at Megan, she was looking slightly better but she knew now that this would only last an hour or two if she was lucky.

'Okay, what are you doing?" Lorna finally asked.

'Waiting for the men in the little white coats to come,' she said calmly.

'What have you done now?'

'I phoned the doctor's and said "It's Mrs Pieters here, may I have an appointment with Dr Gray please". The receptionist asked me to hold on then came back and asked me my name. I couldn't remember what name meant. I thought it can't be Pieters because I've already told her that. I kept saying pardon like I couldn't hear but still couldn't work it out. Well, you can only say 'pardon' so many times before you sound stupid. Finally I said "I'm sorry I've forgotten" and put the phone down! If she

144

dialed 1471 the little men should be here soon.' She roared with laughter and Lorna realised something. She really cared about this woman. She admired her. How the hell did she get into this situation?

'I find it hard to make friends, Lorinda, but you are so easy to talk to.'

Someone else had said that but no, don't think of him.

'My parents didn't want me. It wasn't personal they just didn't like children. They didn't feature in their great life plan,' she confided.

'I'm sure that's not true,' Lorna murmured.

'It's okay, I came to terms with it long ago. They were academics. Their lives were dedicated to work, research and publishing papers. They got a nanny as soon as I was born then we moved to South Africa when I was four. I went to a preprimary school until

I was six. They found a boarding convent and somehow persuaded the nuns to take me as a boarder a few years early. I was the youngest by far so didn't have anything in common with the other girls.'

'That must have been lonely.'

'Yes, terribly at first but you get used to it. The day scholars had activities after school so I didn't make friends with them either. My parents split up when I was eight and they would argue as to who got me for the holidays. The loser got me. Once they forgot it was the school holidays completely and I spent the entire fortnight alone with the nuns. It made me very independent but I know I have a problem relating to people. Cameron was the first person I became friends with, I guess we both mistook that for love. You're the only other person I feel at ease with, I really appreciate your visits. Hey, thirty six years old and I now have two friends, not bad going eh?'

'God, how awful and I thought I had it bad. I had a perfectly normal childhood until my sister came along when I was six. She was premature so needed the extra attention at first. My folks fell totally in love with her, she was so tiny and beautiful. She looked like a little doll. Everyone adored her, even me. She was sweet, girly and graceful, not like me. I guess I always felt second best. Pearl travelled the world then fell in love with a Kiwi and settled in New Zealand. My folks went to visit four times. The last time they only came back long enough to sell up and emigrate. They say they can't afford to come back here for a visit, even when...'

'When what?' Megan asked.

'Oh, um, when I got divorced I could have used

some support but my friends rallied round. They're all happy there and I'm quite happy here. At least I get calls on birthdays and Christmas. Are you still in touch with your parents?'

'No, I think we all sighed in relief when I went off to Uni and they no longer had to put up with me. My father passed away but my mother is still at Stellenbosch as far as I know. Immersed in her study and research, she doesn't really do family or people for that matter.'

'Families really know how to screw you up, don't they? I'm trying to stop my ex from messing my daughter up. She doesn't want to see him anymore and he's threatening me with court if she doesn't.'

'I know a brilliant family advocate if you need one.' Megan scrabbled in a drawer and handed her a business card.

'Thanks for that. Now I'd better go, you're starting to go very pale. To bed with you woman.'

She laughed but toddled off towards her room waving a hand in goodbye.

The weeks went by and Lorna got to know Megan better. She could see now why Cameron was so close to The Android. In fact first impressions are rarely right. Many people put a "face" on to the world. One afternoon Lorna had just put Braeden down for his nap when there was a knock at the door. She opened it and Megan stood there. She froze. Braeden's accoutrements were scattered all over the floor.

'Come in, I'm er… babysitting. Excuse the mess. Would you like a cuppa?' she asked more to give herself time to collect her thoughts than to be hospitable, her mind was racing. She didn't know Megan knew where she lived. she supposed she'd described it a bit too well.

Raven rushed into the kitchen.

'What does she want? Does she know?'

'I don't know, I don't suppose so.'

'I'll do that, you go and find out." Raven said, scuppering her stalling techniques.

'Cameron's away,' Megan said, 'I wanted to ask you round on Saturday night for a thingy…what do you call it?'

'A talk', Lorna suggested.

'Well that too but a whatsit? What is the word?'

'Chat? Visit?'

'No, that thing where I cook and everybody eats it?'

'A meal? Dinner?'

'That's it! Dinner. God awful illness. Will you come to dinner? You're always cooking for me now

I want to cook for you.'

'Are you up to cooking?' Lorna asked.

'Depends on your definition of cooking. Mine is that if you change the state of food from cold to warm then it's cooking. So ready meals for four? You can bring your daughters if you like.'

Lorna had told her she had two daughters but hadn't mentioned Braeden of course. The girls were going out on Saturday so she said it would just be her.

'It's probably better but you girls must come next time.'

It seemed an odd way to put it but sometimes she couldn't find the right words. Lorna offered to bring dessert but Meg wasn't having it. Tesco would do the catering, they even delivered her shopping right to the kitchen. Lorna hadn't been to visit her at night before but it should be okay with Cameron safely away at his conference. Katrin and Amy thought she was nuts to continue this friendship but she was confident she could handle it. She really liked Megan, it was a pity she had to use subterfuge and a fake name to keep the relationship going. She thought Megan got even more out of it than she did as she only had Cameron in her life. Megan said she found it difficult to confide in people but they had just clicked. It wasn't one-sided though, she was warm and funny when you got to know her and had led an interesting life. Okay maybe Lorna did squirrel away little nuggets of information about Cameron but hey, she never said she was perfect. So, dinner party for two on Saturday night it was.

****

CHAPTER SEVEN

Megan is intolerant to alcohol because of the M.E. so Lorna got a bottle of non-alcoholic wine for her and a bunch of flowers. She drew up to their house and noticed the garage door was closed and Megan's car was in the driveway. She was relieved to see no sign of Cameron's. She strode confidently up the drive and knocked on the door.

'I'll get it,' Megan called.

'Sit down, woman, I'll get it.'

Lorna froze. That beautiful voice washed over her. She should turn, run to the car and get the hell out of here but she couldn't move.

'Stop fussing, I can answer a bloody door. I'm not completely decrepit yet.' Megan snapped.

The door opened and they both stood there.

153

Cameron gaped in shock, the blood draining from his face. So he didn't know either.

'Welcome. Come in Lorna.'

Lorna? Lorna? How long had she known? What was this, some kind of game? Payback?

'I can't... I shouldn't... I shouldn't be her, I can't do this,' Lorna stuttered.

'It's just a meal, I got the Tesco gourmet meals, they're quite good apparently.'

Lorna just stared at Megan as Cameron stared at Lorna.

'Come in, for goodness sake. Cameron, help her. Take the wine and flowers, so lovely, thank you Lorna. Now stop standing there like a parrot fish and come in.'

'She went in. Cameron didn't look much better than her, he looked like a stunned trout.

'How do you two…?' he stammered.

Megan was calm, in control almost emotionless. Lorna thought her heart was being ripped out via her throat. He was so beautiful, all the love came surging back almost overwhelming her. Cameron and Lorna peeked at each other furtively, his gorgeous blue eyes so like Braeden's. Lorna wasn't going to start, she hadn't a clue what to say anyway. Cameron was beginning to look more like a halibut, not enough colour in his face to be a trout anymore. Megan ushered them into the dining room and they all sat down. Lorna have never felt more uncomfortable in her life.

'Right. Let's sort this out like intelligent adults. This situation can't go on. Lorna, are you still in love with my husband?'

'I…I'm so sorry…' Where was she going with

this? Was she to be strung up as the evil mistress?

'Cameron and I are friends, best of friends, like I hope you and I are, Lorna,' she looked at him and he smiled at her fondly. 'But we should never have married. It was pleasant, comfortable and a little bit boring actually'.

Lorna looked at Cameron but he was still smiling at Megan.

'I have never seen him so alive, so happy as he was when he was seeing you, Lorna. He loved you, he still does. He's turned into a miserable, boring curmudgeon without you.'

'But…' Cameron tried to interrupt.

'Why the hell should this blasted illness, which has destroyed my life, ruin yours too? You should be together if you still want to be. Now, I know Cameron is going to say I need looking after…'

'You do, honey, I know you hate it but you need caring for, you can't survive on your own. I'm so sorry but nothing has changed.'

Lorna's phone pinged.

'Excuse me,' she said as she read Raven's message.

'STILL ALIVE.'

'It's just Raven, they're on their own tonight and she knows I worry. I understand, Cameron, I know how ill Megan is.'

'You've both been looking after me for the last few months. Why can't you still do that without living with me?'

'You're Lorinda?' Cameron asked.

'Just a private joke,' Megan insisted.

'You're the one who found her that day? You've been looking after her when I go away? Why?'

Cameron asked.

'It's okay. I'm not some creepy stalker. I found her that day and despite my better judgement brought her home. I was so worried I came back the next day to see how she was. I started popping in and we got on. I liked her. She's a devious old hag but I liked her although that is subject to change.' She glared at Megan.

'See,' Megan said smugly. 'She liked me. Hey, why is it past tense?'

'I'm not sure after your shenanigans tonight. What the hell are you playing at? I nearly had a heart attack when I saw him at the door.' Lorna smiled.

'I thought I was seeing a ghost. I was expecting Lorinda. Imagine how I felt?' Cameron said.

'Let's get the food on the table and talk this through before I start flaking out.' Megan suggested.

'That's just it Meg. You are still very ill.'

'I'm not completely helpless.'

'This from the woman who couldn't stand up last week. She sat in the shower, frozen and in pain, until I got home a few hours later.' He smiled at Megan affectionately. 'She's so fiercely independent, fights all offers of help. She insists on doing the shopping online. We are now the proud owners of eight bottles of tomato sauce and enough vinegar to last a fish and chip shop a month…. with enough left over to clean all the windows at Buckingham Palace. I wouldn't mind so much but neither of us like tomato sauce.'

'It was only six bottles of vinegar,' Megan pouted.

'Yes, but we only get through about a cupful a year.'

'That's not the point. The point is you two love each other so why can't you have a relationship?

159

And I think Lorna and I are now friends?' she looked at Lorna who nodded. 'I'm not saying I don't need help and I know I have difficulty in asking for it. I'm not saying you should ride off into the sunset and forget me. Can't I just ask for help when I need it?'

'You won't.' Cameron replied.

'I will.'

'You won't.'

'I promise I will.'

'Megan, if you chopped your arm off and blood was spurting everywhere you would say you were fine. God, I still have nightmares about that day I found you. I was on a walk, happy as Larry when my phone rang. I thought it was you Lorna then I saw Megan's name. She couldn't talk though.'

He had hesitated a moment his finger poised, hovering over his phone then snapped it back into his pocket and ran to his car. His brow was crenelated with worry. He raced round to his former home, parked the car haphazardly and rushed to the door. He rang the bell and banged the door with his fist. Hands shaking slightly he found the no- longer-used key on the ring and shoved in into the door. He wrenched it open and loped inside.

She lay on the floor, the phone still in her hand. Unaccustomed tears ran down her ashen face.

He grabbed the phone, 'What is it? Heart attack? Stroke? I'll call an ambulance.' He kept the panic at bay as his mind ran through the correct sequence of airway, breathing, pulse.

'Nooo,' she slurred, 'bed, tired, dizzy.'

'You need to go to hospital, see a doctor,' he stated calmly.

'Seen one, just need bed.'

He stared at her, this woman he had been married to, the one he'd never seen cry, so strong, so self-sufficient, so fiercely independent. Then he lifted her in his arms and carried her to the bedroom like a child. His heart thudded in fear and confusion.

He spent the night in the spare room, checking on Megan regularly. She slept through the next day and night. The following day she was a lot brighter. She explained that she'd been to hospital and been through a barrage of tests. They thought she'd been ill for at least a year but now it had become severe.

'I haven't been able to do the things I used to do and have had a lot of time off work,' she explained.

'Why didn't you tell me?'

'Cameron, I have to live my own life now, I'm not your responsibility.'

'I thought we were friends, Meg, friends for life.

162

I'm always here for you. I'm moving back and that's all there is to it, Megan,' Cameron said.

'Don't be ridiculous. I'm fine. You can't put your life on hold for me. What about whatshername? Your girlfriend? I'm sure she'll be happy for you to move in with your ex-wife.'

'You're not fine, you're ill, really ill and for the first time in your life you have to let people help you, to let me help you. Come on, Megan, we're best friends, aren't we? I wouldn't leave a dog in the state you're in. Lorna will understand. And I'll be in the spare room.'

'I can manage. Always have, always will. I don't do "illness", remember? I'm sure I'll get over this in no time and don't need you to nanny me. 'I'm strong,' Megan whispered, 'I can do it on my

own.....tomorrow. If you could just help me to bed now though, please.'

'There's a treatment then?'

'Not exactly. Okay there's no treatment and no cure'

Cameron shook his head to rid the memories of that awful day. The day he felt wrenched in two between the love and loyalty he had for the two women.

'Oh, you managed fine when you collapsed in the fridge full of cherries in Tesco last week, didn't you? Some days you can't even get to the bathroom without help. Stop being so bloody stubborn. Look at you, you're even too tired to argue with me aren't you?'

Lorna started to think she had blundered in to centre court at Wimbledon by mistake. They continued their gentle, teasing argument whilst she remained the spectator. Megan admitted that she needed a little help, graduating to admitting she needed a lot of help. Cameron conceded grudgingly, that he may be a little over-protective.

'If Lorna is still willing to call in and see me sometimes, especially when you're away then I don't see why it won't work. She's only ten minutes down the road. And you could pop in every night after work, if Lorna doesn't mind. Right, that's me sorted out now how about you two? Will you be wanting to move out straight away, Cameron? Or you could *continue* to stay in the little spare room for a while?' Megan asked tentatively as Lorna's butterflies awoke and started to flutter in some hope at the words "continue" and "spare room". So he hadn't really got back together with her then.

'I don't even know if Lorna wants me back with all the complications.'

'Of course she does. Didn't you see her face when she spotted you at the door?'

'Meg you can't always railroad people into doing what you want.'

'This is so surreal. A wife is not supposed to try and get her husband back with his girlfriend.' Lorna interjected.

Meg's face fell. 'You don't want him back? But he's lovely, he's kind and generous, funny but not as funny as he thinks he is. And he really loves you, don't you Cameron.'

'Meg, I think I can be trusted to hold that conversation on my own, thanks.'

'I've got some complications of my own that I need to discuss with you, Cameron, alone. You may not want me back. Of course, I'll still help you out, Meg, no matter what happens. I'm still on m... I work a lot from home now. I think Cameron and I have a lot to talk about.'

'Of course he wants you back. You could take her for dinner again at that lovely Piper Dam, Cameron. Why don't you do that tomorrow. But now let's eat. We have lasagna but the Tesco luxury brand, special treat, I'll go and dish up.' Megan rose and left the table.

'Do you need help?' Cameron asked.

'No," she snapped then gentler 'no, I'm fine for now. I don't think I'll be redecorating the kitchen in pasta tonight. You could open a bottle of wine. I'm sure Lorna would like a glass. It'll be nice for you to have someone to drink with again. Alcohol doesn't go with M.E. Can't even drown my sorrows. Still it does make me slur, stagger, have double vision and repeat myself as though I'm drunk so who am I to complain?'

Lorna was beginning to understand why Cameron loved this woman so much. She knew how ill Megan was and didn't think she could handle it as well as her never mind joke about it. She could appear cold and hard with her professional veneer but underneath she was brave and funny. Lorna thought she was growing to love her too.

'I brought you a bottle of non-alcoholic wine, I'll join you Megan as I'm driving." She couldn't mention breast-feeding, could she?

'Schloer. Shlooo er. Funny name for non-alcoholic wine, makes you think you're drunk just pronouncing it.' Megan grinned.

Lorna's phone went again, Raven was having fun.

'AMAZING! CALL THE PRESS. WE ARE STILL ALIVE.'

Megan came through with three plates of lasagna on a tray. She handed theirs to them.

'I've had enough company and talking for one night. Please excuse me, I need some quiet and banal television. I've become quite addicted to the box, I can only watch light things but it can just wash over me and I don't have to concentrate or talk back. Good night, Lorna, sorry for ambushing you. I'm so glad you came, he deserves some happiness.'

They were tentative at first, pussyfooting around. It was strange trying to kick-start a relationship with his wife not only upstairs but the instigator of the whole thing. They didn't talk much but Lorna's smile was getting so wide it was difficult getting her fork in her mouth. He was just as bad, grinning at her idiotically. Those lovely blue eyes were dancing with joy. His hand crept over and covered then gripped hers. They couldn't let go. It's not that easy eating lasagna one-handed.

'Is this really happening? I'm not going to wake up heartbroken all over again, am I?' Cameron whispered.

'Were you? Heartbroken?'

'Every morning when I woke up and remembered that you weren't in my life.'

They finally finished the meal and Lorna rose to leave. He went to kiss her but she stopped him. She wanted to get all obstacles hurdled- over first. Maybe he'd never wanted children. Maybe he'd be so angry that she didn't tell him straight away when she found out she was pregnant that he would want nothing to do with her. Maybe he wouldn't want three kids in his life. But in those seconds at the door, before reality struck, when he first saw her his face had lit with joy. Lorna retrieved her hand, sat down again and clutched her wine glass and took a very deep breath.

'I have to tell you a few things first. My life has changed a lot recently,' she said.

'You said you're working from home now?'

'Yes, Paul opened a new branch in Cupar which I am running. I have some staff so I can work from home sometimes. Do you remember Tamaryn? Raven's friend. Her parents had to move to London and she didn't want to interrupt her schooling so she moved in with us.'

'Yes, of course I remember Tams, a lovely kid.'

'Her phone pinged.

"WE ARE ACTUALLY BREATHING!" the text read. She smiled then turned her attention back to Cameron.

'And…' she couldn't carry on.

'And what, love? Come on, it's me, you can tell me anything. Have you met someone else? Is that it?'

She dragged some more air into her lungs and clutched the wineglass to her chest. 'No, never. But, I didn't know. I swear I didn't know, not for a long time and then I saw her and she was just the same. I mean exactly the same, she looked fine and I thought. I thought…"

'You're losing me, darling. Who looked the same? Take your time.'

'I saw Megan. She looked well, the same as I'd seen her before, striding down the street, looking healthy. I thought....I thought you'd been lying to me all along, that there was nothing wrong with her and I'd just been your bit on the side which is why I didn't tell you.'

'That must have been a shock for you. It's the nature of her illness, sometimes she looks awful but most of the time she looks perfectly healthy even though she feels like death slightly de-frosted. When you know her well you can tell the signs, the rings around her eyes get darker and her eyes are dull.'

'Yes, I've noticed that, her eyes look kind of glazed and hooded. You can tell she doesn't really know what's going on but I didn't know her then. I thought you just used me. I didn't think you deserved to know.'

'To know what?' he demanded. She could see the cogs starting to turn.

'I honestly didn't know myself for months. I was so upset when we split up and I was eating more rubbish. It was such a shock when I found out. I didn't know what to do…'

'Are you ill too? Is there something wrong? Just tell me, darling, it's okay, whatever it is.'

'She closed her eyes then blurted 'Cameron, I'm so sorry. I had your baby, my… our son.' She almost whispered the last words.

There was silence, a deep empty silence. She opened one eye. He was shocked, absolutely, totally shocked but as his brain decoded her words into the right order the most amazing smile she have ever seen stretched his mouth until she thought it would split.

'We have a baby boy, a son? Oh my God. We really have a baby? I'm a daddy? I'm really a daddy?

You should have told me. Oh Lorna, you went through it all on your own.'

'I had the coven and Raven and Tams. Tams was brilliant.'

'Raven, Tamaryn and....?'

'Braeden Pieters Robson. I've gone back to my maiden name and Raven wants to be known as Robson too. No doubt that will cause more fights with John but right now I just wanted to concentrate on my beautiful boy and girls.'

'You gave him my name. I can't believe I have a son. You wonderful, beautiful, daft woman.' He grabbed her, she saw the wine spill in an arc as her glass fell to the floor as if in slow motion. He swept her into his arms and danced her round the room, whooping like a little boy.

'Ssh! You'll wake Megan. You'll have to break it

to her gently.'

'Gently? She'll be over the moon. Meg! Meg! I'm a daddy! We've got a baby boy,' he called.

A very changed Megan shuffled into the room. This was more like the woman Lorna had found in Dundee. Her eyes were sunk in black rings and her face was ashen yet still she raised a smile.

'My love, I'm so happy for you. Does that mean I'm an uncle? A step-brother? ..Mother, I mean. Sort of in reverse, can't work it out right now. Going back to bed but I'm happy for you both. You had a baby. I'm truly, truly happy for you but can you shut up and piss off and leave me to sleep. I'll be much happier for you tomorrow, I promise.'

They shut up and Cameron took her tenderly back to bed. He made her some Milo in hot milk and switched off the lights as he came back.

'The lights hurt her eyes,' he whispered. 'Can I see him? Sorry, when can I see him?'

Lorna's phone pinged again.

'IT'S A MIRACLE!! HE'S STILL BREATHING.'

She showed it to Cameron.

'It's the first time I've left the girls completely alone with him in the evening. No doubt Mrs Mac is creeping around the garden, keeping an eye on them. You're not going to wait another second are you?'

'Nope, I shall follow you home and peer through the curtains with my ultra-zoom lens if you don't take me right now. I reckon I would make quite a good stalker if I put my mind to it.'

They set off in Lorna's car, she didn't trust him to drive.

'STOP!' Cameron pounded on the dashboard.

Lorna performed the perfect emergency stop, her old driving instructor would have been proud.

'Tesco. I can't go to meet my son empty handed. Drive to Tesco, woman.'

She turned the car round and headed over the bridge to Dundee. She texted Raven, while she waited, to let her know they would both be home soon. After an eternity a trolley approached the car, apparently being pushed by a six foot Winnie-the-Pooh. A blue bunny was sitting atop piles of baby goods and roughly all the bunches of flowers the shop possessed. They filled the boot and the entire back seat. Not having yet been in close contact with a baby before, and having failed to ask Braeden's age Cameron had bought one of every item a baby could possibly want in every size ranging from premature to two years old. Thank goodness Tesco have a good returns policy.

They arrived at the cottage and he gripped Lorna's hand hard as she opened the door. The girls had changed Braeden from his Babygro into his smartest outfit, a little sailor suit, while he slumbered on. With a look of awe in his eyes, Cameron gazed at his son for the first time. He cradled him gently in his large hands. As though he knew what a momentous occasion it was, Braeden opened his deep, blue eyes and gazed back then smiled up at his father. Cameron, solemnly introduced himself to his son.

When Raven was born Lorna supposed she was consumed with her own feelings, the pain, the fear, the feelings of profound responsibility and deep maternal love. John had loved her in his own, odd way but to Lorna it was always as a possession, as an

179

extension of himself. You had to constantly earn John's love. It was never enough to just be yourself. She was delighted to see that overpowering rush of pure love, which she had felt at both her children's births, mirrored now in Cameron's eyes. Yet still he remembered to turn to Raven and give her a hug, telling her how much he had loved and missed her. Tamaryn too, was enveloped in his arms but just before it turned mawkish he tickled them and had a cushion fight while Braeden chuckled.

****

CHAPTER EIGHT

Cameron moved quickly. He put his house on the market, rented a flat for Megan in Cupar and once she was settled he moved in with Lorna. The girls were going to London for the weekend to visit Tammy's parents and brothers so it was just Cameron, Braeden and Lorna. They had a wonderfully romantic weekend and father and son had many bonding sessions. Braeden was nearly six months old and was very interested in this strange male in the household. The first time he said 'Dadad' Cameron was so choked up he couldn't speak and just hugged his son tightly.

One of them called in every day to care for Megan. The coven moved their Wednesday girls' night to her flat that she could join them then toddle off to bed when she'd had enough. They started having dinner there as they had to finish earlier to get Raven and Tamaryn home at a reasonable hour for school the next day. Amy didn't come very often though. Lorna rang her.

'Amy, is it a problem for you having Megan there? She's really not as bad as you thought. It takes her a long time to get to know people enough to trust them and open up. Give her a chance. She's really funny and warm once she lets her guard down.'

'It's not that, it's just…Duncan isn't keen on me driving to Cupar.'

'It's only 3 miles further than my house and Katrin alternates driving with you.'

'I know but he likes me to be there for dinner and sometimes he has work dos he wants me to go with him.'

'Well, okay, Amy as long as everything is okay and you will really like Megan when you get to know her properly.'

Katrin was livid. 'It's only one evening a week for goodness sake. She says she'll come then when I go to pick her up it's one excuse after another.'

'Maybe it's her thingy,' Megan mused.

'Her thingy?' they cried in unison.

'Her whatdoyoumacallit. Maybe he won't let her come.'

'Duncan? No. He adores her, would do anything for her,' Lorna said.

'Maybe a bit too much. Is he possessive?' Meg asked.

'Hadn't really thought about it. I would say they're both so into each other they're still on honeymoon after a couple of years together.'

183

'Humm,' was all Megan said.

Lorna knew what it was like to hide secrets behind closed doors. Was Amy unhappy? She had seemed much quieter recently and she was cancelling a lot of their get-togethers. Maybe an idea to keep an eye on her. Cameron had a meeting that night and Tammy and Raven elected to babysit. So it was just Megan, Katrin and Lorna.

'What do you think about sex?' Megan threw into the conversation like a primed grenade.

'What?' Katrin and Lorna cried in unison.

'You know, sex,' Megan said tentatively, 'what do you think about it?'

'I am NOT having a conversation with you about sex,' Lorna said. 'I'm sleeping with your husband for God's sake.'

'Ex,' Megan replied.

'And I don't think she does it for God's sake either although his name may be called at some stage in the proceedings,' Kat smirked. 'What do you want to know?'

'Well, it's not like it is in books and films is it? They exaggerate all that huffing and puffing and thrashing about, don't they? I mean sex is nice and all that but....'

'Sex ISN'T nice,' Kat retorted. 'It's wild and passionate.'

'Romantic and silly,' Lorna added.

'Mind-blowing and dull.'

'Tender and hysterically funny.'

'Comforting, messy and fun.'

'Warm and gentle, the epitome of love.'

'Joyous and earth-shattering. The most fun you can have lying down, or standing up, or in the shower or...'

'Okay Kat, we get the picture. Megan how many men have you slept with?' Lorna asked gently before Kat could corrupt her completely.

'Um....er...one.'

'Bloody hell! Lorna I thought you said Cameron was great in bed.'

'He is, we... I can't talk about it with Megan." Lorna blushed.

'You see, I wanted to know if there was something wrong with me. I mean it was pleasant but I've never had an orgasm. So if Lorna is happy it must be me. I must have been doing it wrong,'

'Oh, Meg, you've just not had enough experience. Both you and Cameron said you were more like brother and sister when you were married. Is that really true?' Lorna asked gently.

'I've never loved anyone except Cam but it was nothing like the butterflies everyone talks about. I could never understand when people said 'it just happened'. I mean how do you get all your clothes off and it just happens? It takes time. Surely you could stop and think while you're getting undressed?'

'Not when you're ripping them off,' Kat smirked. 'If you really felt like that about Cam then it would be very peculiar to feel sexy about your brother. We need to find you a man.'

'It's too late for that now,' Megan sighed. 'I don't think I could now. The slightest exertion makes me ill for days, sometimes weeks.'

'Then you lie back and let him do all the work.' Kat replied.

Lorna felt sorry for Megan but at the same time she was glad to know Meg and Cam had told her the truth. They'd had a very odd, almost platonic, relationship. It seemed that neither of them had met 'the one', they'd just fallen into a comfortable rut with each other. She did vow to go home and make sure that Cameron did not think sex was just "nice" though. By the grin on his face she gathered that she had succeeded.

As Lorna was leaving to pop into the office Raven called out, 'Megan called, she asks if you could get her a cheap, pay-as-you-go mobile.'

'What's happened to her phone?'

'I don't know, I didn't ask.'

Lorna checked in with Maureen and picked up some work to take home. She bought the mobile and called in at Megan's flat.

'Firemen are jolly nice, aren't they?'

'I suppose so, haven't really met any personally.

How did you meet them?'

'I was making lunch. I realised something was wrong when I found the trout in my pocket.'

'What?'

'It seems I put my mobile in the microwave and my lunch in my pocket. The firemen were really understanding. I'll need to order another microwave oven though.'

'What are we going to do with you? You can't be left alone for a minute!'

'You try living without a brain and see how well you get on! At least I've still got fish for lunch.'

They fell into a comfortable routine and Lorna grew ever closer to Megan. Cameron was a man of action and still felt Megan was too far away from them. She was having a bit of trouble with noisy neighbours which became increasingly difficult as she had to sleep so much. She was being woken

morning and night. She wasn't coping with cooking

even disregarding the mobile incident. Most days she

would just have toast or a sandwich. They also had

the problem of finding an extra room as Braeden was

now sleeping in the living room. They just wheeled

his cot back and forth. When the neighbours in the

other semi mentioned they also wanted to move to a

larger place he turned into the estate agent on speed.

He found out exactly what they wanted and searched

the listings for them until he found their dream

home. The money had come through from the sale of

his and Megan's house so he worked his charm on

the landlord and they bought both semis.

'I can't live with you,' Megan objected. 'How can

we all live together, me, my ex and his girlfriend?'

But the man had a plan. He decided as Megan

couldn't cook anymore that we would have a communal kitchen and knocked down the dividing wall. He incorporated Megan's living room into our house, giving us another bedroom and converted her spare room into a cosy, little living room for her. The cottages were built with huge, thick stone walls so no noise from Braeden or the girls could penetrate them. They were single storey too so no stairs for Megan to negotiate. By September the work was all done and Megan was settled into her little cottage. She had the peace and beauty of the countryside with plenty of carers on hand to help her. Lorna supposed it was odd to outsiders but it worked for them.

Lorna was back working mornings and bringing work home in the afternoon. Mrs Mac insisted on looking after Braeden.

'Och, It's a delight looking after the wee mannie.

We go for a walk every morning and he loves watching the birds at the feeder. On a sunny day he recognizes the first clop on the road and starts wriggling and screaming in delight. I have to run outside with him to watch the riders and their horses go by. They always have a wee chat with him and let him stroke the horses. He keeps me young. Every lining has a silver cloud.'

The peremptory knock on the door gave Lorna an idea who it might be. She opened the door.

'John.'

'Lorna. I demand to see my daughter.'

'I told you before, John, I don't want you to come to my home. We can talk about Raven anywhere else.'

'Do not dictate to me about when and where I can see my daughter. This place,' he sneered, 'is her home and I am entitled to see her here. Get her.'

Cameron appeared at her shoulder.

'You heard the lady, leave now. And never speak to her like that again. Lorna is the mother of your child and should be spoken to respectfully.'

'You must be the boyfriend, father of the bastard.'

Lorna feared she would have to restrain Cameron. Just then Megan came stumbling through in her nightie.

'Who the hell is that?' John demanded.

'I,' Megan said with a wicked gleam in her eye, 'am the wife. You must be the bastard ex. You are disturbing my rest.'

'Christ, what kind of depravity is going on here?'

'Bye, John.' Lorna closed the door in his face. She knew he wouldn't pursue the issue with Cameron there. It was women John liked to bully not a man likely to punch him.

The following week a letter arrived from John's lawyer. Not only was he demanding access to Raven he was now applying for full custody due to the 'depravity' of her home situation. Raven was hysterical and Lorna wasn't much better. Cameron did his best to calm them all down. Megan phoned her friend, the Family Advocate and made an appointment.

Megan decided to join the local ME support group. She learned a lot about her illness and they all learned about pacing. Apparently because she suffered from something called Post Exertional Malaise she had to cut everyday tasks into tiny segments and have rest periods in between. This included talking, watching television as well as more physical tasks. Lorna had thought 'exertion' was a game of squash or hoofing it up a hill at Cameron's speed but with ME everything was an exertion, even thinking. Tammy and Raven became her taskmasters using the alarms on their phones to make sure she stuck to the regime. It was rather shocking living in close proximity with her and realizing how devastating the illness is.

Some days she was her normal intelligent self but at other times she couldn't string a sentence together. One morning Lorna found her in the kitchen, the kettle had just boiled but she was just standing there.

'I don't know what to do – don't tell me. I want to work it out myself. If I pour the water in the sugar bowl the sugar will melt, I don't want that. If I pour it in the milk I'll get hot, watery milk, I don't want that.'

Her face lit with a smile.

'I know! I pour it in the mug.'

She looked into the mug and her face fell. 'I'm sure I put a teabag in here.'

Gently, Lorna pointed to her bowl. Next to it lay the spoon and milk. The bowl was filled with cereal and sitting neatly, and proudly, on top was a tea bag.

She found a lot of support at the group. She said it was amazing to find people who understood exactly what she was going through. One of them would start speaking and before they had finished the sentence, the others were nodding agreement. Although relatively new to the illness, some people had suffered for decades, her practical no-nonsense nature and sense of humour meant she could help others too.

Lorna tapped on the communal kitchen door and went in. Megan was on the phone and waved hello. Lorna listened to her side of the conversation with awe.

'What you do, when people come to view the house, is tell them they're in for a treat, fling the door open with an enthusiastic ta-dah and wait for their stunned silence. Point to the half-stripped walls and say: "Isn't it marvelous? It was designed by Jasper Woollington-Pumphrey. Oh, it will break my heart to leave it. The distressed look is sooo fashionable now. Doesn't it just scream of the joy and sorrow of the fragile human condition?" Then take them to your best-decorated room and shake your head sadly and say: "I'm so sorry about this room. Jasper didn't have time to do this room but as an enormous favour he is designing our entire new house, isn't that simply wonderful?'

Lorna heard laughter coming through the phone.

Megan continued with a smile, 'Then you say:

197

'You know I'm sure that if I pleaded him very nicely he would put you at the end of his very long waiting list. Besides being beautiful (*give a big wink or nudge here if you can*), it will add enormously to the value of the house although you'll be glad to know, of course, that I haven't incorporated it into MY asking price seeing as only one room is done."

'It'll work a treat. Of course I don't know Jasper Woollington-Pumphrey I just made him up. People always want to know they're getting something the common herd can't. Got to go now, let me know how you get on. Bye.'

Megan put the phone down with a wicked grin.

'What are you up to now?' Lorna asked.

'One of my ME friends is having to sell her house, she's down-sizing to a smaller place with no steps. She half-stripped the wallpaper in the hall five years ago and hasn't had the energy to do any more since. I told her to make it a selling point.' She chuckled.

'Where does she live?'

'Just outside Newburgh.

'We could get the gang together to strip the paper and give it a lick of paint. I'm sure Mrs Mac would baby-sit.'

'You're very kind.' Megan said.

'Oh nonsense,' Lorna muttered, 'why do people keep saying that, although most say it as though it's a peculiar character trait.'

'Because kind people are few and far between, sadly. There are so many people isolated in their own homes with no-one to help. I'm so lucky to have you lot. I can't think of anyone who would want the ex-wife hanging around let alone caring for her, washing, dressing, cooking for her. Now you're doing it for my friends. Dammit now my eyes are leaking!'

'It's called crying Meg and it's allowed. God knows if I had to put up with what you do I'd probably be crying all the time. Any way I'm not the greatest decorator but at least the hall would look fresh.'

'I'll tell Mhairi but I was rather looking forward to hearing how Jasper got on. I'd just love someone to take the bait. I could babysit,' she said hopefully.

'Megan, it's very tiring, I think you'd last an hour at most. I'm sure Mrs Mac would do it.'

The next Friday Lorna, Cameron, the two girls and even Kat dressed in their oldest clothes and descended on Newburgh. Once again Amy couldn't join them. Mhairi was a sweet woman who was slightly worse than Megan. They sent her off to her elderly mother's house for the weekend and started stripping the old paper off. Cameron had hired one of those heat machines so it went quite quickly. By Sunday evening they were all exhausted but every room had a fresh coat of paint.

****

CHAPTER NINE

A week later Lorna got a strange call from Gladys.

'I'm sorry to bother you, pet, but I've got a message for you and young Joel's off with the flu, poor thing, and Maureen's off seeing a client. It's a bitty urgent and well, I don't really know what to say,' she was in a fluster.

'That's okay, Gladys, just give me the message.'

'I can't do that.'

'Gladys, who was it and what did they say?'

'Well, it's a bit delicate, could you come to the office? I don't know who it was that left the message but it was a man's voice, I think,' she finished hopefully.

'Gladys I don't think I need to come down for a

message when you don't know who it is or who it's from. I'm sure Maureen will handle it when she comes back."

'No, he definitely mentioned you and it's urgent and I can't do it on the phone.'

She sounded close to tears. The girls were at school, Cameron was at work so it was just Megan at home. She assured Lorna that she could watch Braeden for a short while so Lorna drove down to the office.

Gladys was very agitated and led her to her office where she practically force-fed her some lukewarm, sickly sweet tea.

'It's good for shock.'

'But I haven't had a shock yet.'

'You will. I didn't want to break it to you over the phone. I'm sorry to have to inform you that someone has died,' she said solemnly.

'Who?'

'Well, I don't really know but he was phoning to inform you.'

'Was the call from abroad? My dad or brother-in-law?'

'I don't rightly know. He was rambling a bittie,' she said sorrowfully.

'Did he leave a number? Has anyone phoned since, maybe we could find out from the last number recall.'

'Um, no, I didn't get the number and we've had a couple of calls since. I wrote them down,' she said proudly.

'Gladys, take a deep breath and try to relax. Now tell me everything you remember him saying.'

'He said she'd died at the weekend. Something

about wood....and you and the coffin.'

Lorna struggled not to laugh.

'Was it perhaps that he had to cancel his appointment with me because he had a coffin to prepare for a funeral? Could it have been Mr MacLeod the undertaker?'

'That's who it was lass. I knew I recognized that sombre voice from somewhere. So you didn't know her?'

'Who?'

'The deceased.'

'Not as far as I know, Gladys. He was supposed to meet me so we could go over his books. Don't look so upset, he's got a weird sense of humour and may have been winding you up deliberately. You know he goes into the pub at night, sidles up to someone and asks them how they are. When they reply 'fine', he responds with 'that's a pity' and walks off.'

'Oh he's some man!'

'Just in future, Gladys, if you have to answer the phone, grab a notepad and pen first, take a deep breath then answer and write down the name and phone number. They won't ring off straight away and if it's important they will ring back. Now could I have a hot cuppa with less than a bowlful of sugar in it please?'

Lorna returned home and found Braeden and Meg having a nap together. She tiptoed back into her side of the house. There was a bunch of flowers on the table. She lifted them and read the card: To Lorna and Raven, I'm sorry. John.

She'd never had flowers from John before. And he'd never, ever said he was sorry about anything. They made her feel disconcerted. She stood looking between the vase and the bin, not sure which receptacle was the more appropriate.

'That was quick.'

Lorna jumped at Megan's voice.

'What do you mean?'

'I had an interesting visit while you were out. It turns out the man understands English better when it's spoken by another Android. God, was I really as bad as him? I've had more fun talking to my toaster. He's dropping the custody case and has agreed to see Raven for an hour with supervision.'

'He was here again? How…. How the hell did you manage that?'

'I sat him down and told him how screwed up he was. I told him how screwed up I was and how living here with your family has changed me. I told him how successful I was in my career, just like him, and how hated I was. How empty my life was. Then I asked him if that was truly the life he wanted for Raven. I told him how bright and funny and kind his daughter is and did he really want to destroy that. I said many people get damaged by their parents but once you're an adult you're supposed to be able to think for yourself and break the cycle. Because you had bad parents didn't mean you have to be one yourself. Look at you. Your parents show obvious favouritism to your sister but you love and treat Tams the same as Raven. I said Raven was fifteen now and I doubted he could undo all the good work you'd done on her in just a year. Then I told him how lonely and miserable he was going to be when he lost her for good in a year's time, not only losing her but any grandchildren she may have.'

'You said all that and you're still alive?' Lorna

was stunned.

'We decided that to build bridges he would only see Raven for an hour a week with me as chaperone. I told him I would cut it short every time he said anything critical or negative towards her. He may be an autocratic machine but deep down he does love her.'

'Wow, Meg, just wow. Thank you.' Lorna hugged her tight.

'Ouch.'

'Sorry, Meg. It's not fair this pigging illness. I can't even give you a hug without hurting you. You're so great it's not fair that you got this.'

'I never, ever thought I would find a positive in ME. Feeling ill and in pain every minute of every day and I think my brain has packed its bags and moved to Outer Mongolia, but we would never have become friends if you hadn't found me that day. And I wouldn't get to share your family.'

'You are family, Meg. We all love you.'

'Oh shut up you mawkish cow, you'll have my eyes leaking again.'

'Crying.'

'I'm the Android, I don't cry, my eyes just leak. Now go and make me a cuppa I can hear the young master waking.'

Meg was true to her word and as soon as John slipped back into his controlling, critical ways she threw him out. And he left, sheepishly. It was amazing to see. He even started arriving tieless and with the top button of his shirt undone. That was ultra-casual wear to him. Slowly Raven learned to trust her dad until she was happy to see him on her own or with Tammy in tow.

One day Cam came home and announced he had a surprise for Meg. A van arrived and hooted outside. They all trooped out to see what it was. The man opened the van and brought out a shiny, red, mobility scooter. Megan's jaw clenched. She obediently underwent the instructions and lessons. The girls thought it was brilliant and took turns scooting up and down the road. Braeden thought all his Christmases had come at once and was soon ensconced on Meg's lap as she reluctantly took him for rides. As soon as she decently could she muttered a thank you and stomped inside. By now she was using two canes for support so it was difficult to stomp but she did her best and her rigid spine and shoulders told the rest of the story.

'How dare you! I'm only in my thirties and you want me in a glorified wheelchair. I've been in one of

211

them and I hated it. I told you, Cameron. Everyone treated me like a moron. No-one spoke to me, they spoke to the person pushing me.' She hissed at Cameron as soon as they got inside.

'This is different. It's to give you some of your independence back, Meg. On a nice day you can go for 'walks' up the road, go and see the lambs, enjoy the scenery and fresh air.'

'Just don't tell me fresh air will make me better,' she snapped.

'I'm not Megan, I wouldn't, but you used to enjoy walking in the country. I thought it would conserve your energy too so you can use it for enjoyable things. And perhaps not get the back pay.'

'Payback. Just going out for a cup of tea in a café for half an hour means I'll be bedbound for days afterwards.'

212

'But this way you won't be walking so the payback might not be as bad. Maybe you won't do your dying swan things in shops any more. You say you're only dizzy when you're standing up so it might not be so bad sitting on the scooter. And when you get the sensitive thing..'

'Sensory overload.'

'Yes, sensory overload from all the noise, lights and movement, you could get yourself out quicker to somewhere quiet. You saw how easy it is to break down and put in the car, I think you could handle it on your own. I got the lightest one on the market. You could drive into town alone and zoot around on your scooter.'

'I'm still young, it's older people on these things. People glare at me for using my Blue Badge and say I'm too young to be disabled. As if.'

'Since when do you care about what strangers think about you?'

She still wasn't convinced but allowed Lorna to take her and the scooter shopping in the Overgate, Dundee. As soon as they got it out of the car two women crossed the road to exclaim how marvelous it was. They split up and went in different directions. When they met at the café for coffee Megan had a slight flush to her cheeks.

'I went to six shops. Six! I haven't done that in years.'

Normally she only had the energy to visit one shop and that was only if she could get parking at the door.

'You know what's the best? Whizzing past all the old pensioners. I've got nothing against them, bless them, but it was soul-destroying when they outpaced

me on their zimmer frames. And people chatted to
me all the time, not like when I was in the
wheelchair. I guess because it's electric and I operate
it myself they think I must have some brain cells.
When I walk I have to concentrate so hard on not
falling on my face that my best friend could walk
past and I wouldn't notice.'

'I thought I was your best friend,' Lorna grinned.

'Okay, YOU could walk past and I wouldn't
notice but now I can look around and see people I
know. Even strangers say "hello". It makes me feel
part of the world again.'

It wasn't a cure by any means but it meant she
wasn't stuck in the house so much and didn't suffer
so badly afterwards. It helped her pace better. She
bravely let Raven and Tams loose on it and they
soon had it customized. Stars and gems glittered on

the tiller and ribbons streamed from the handle bars. Lorna got her a bag which fitted on the back of the seat.

Megan had seen all the doctors and specialists available to her but the latter always sent her back to her GP saying 'It's ME, there's nothing we can do.' She was told the only viable therapy was Graded Exercise. It didn't make any sense to her as she hadn't just stopped doing things overnight, nor did she do it on a whim. As the weeks and months had gone by she had found she could do less and less without suffering dreadful payback. She was desperate to get well again so she hauled herself down to the Physiotherapy department.

There were twenty people with ME in her group. They were told that riding an exercise bike with no tension was easier than walking. She was so happy and excited to be doing exercise again, she absolutely loved it. The first week she spent entirely in bed, barely able to eat but on the Thursday morning she dragged herself out of bed and was ready, waiting for the ambulance car to pick her up. By the second week five people had dropped out of the group. Megan was determined that she was going to make it.

Lorna, Cameron and Braeden went away for a long planned mini break in the fourth week, they left on Tuesday and were due back on Friday afternoon. They went to Alnwick Lodge in Northumbria. Lorna had found this unique B & B, just a three hour drive from home. On arrival the owner greeted them with a tray of tea, coffee and biscuits served in front of a roaring fire in the communal lounge. Some other guests were already ensconced there and the conversation soon flowed.

The beautiful courtyard was filled with shrubs, flowers and creepers. A large table made from the axle and wheel from a cart was where the guests gathered whenever the sun shone. Although it was just off the A1, the horseshoe shape of the building sheltered them from traffic noise so it felt like a peaceful oasis. They were settled into their room, the Mouse House. Every room was unique and, as the owners also ran an antique business, all the pictures, ornaments and even furniture was for sale. They put a cot in the room for Braeden but he just wanted to get back to the antique rocking horse in the lounge. In the morning breakfast was served at three huge, round tables in the dining room, the former stables. Between the tables were genuine partitions from the stables with a few hoof-shaped dents in them. Lorna found at most B & B's people would greet each other in the morning and that was it. But at Alnwick everyone chatted to each other. In the morning they would all discuss where they were going for the day and in the evening they all gathered outside or around the fire to chat about their day and where the best places for evening meals were.

Braeden charmed all the guests and fell in love with the farm kitten. It was great to have time away with Cameron and she could feel her batteries recharging. On Thursday morning they set off for Alnwick Castle where the Harry Potter films were made. After many photographs and jokes about quiddich, they set off to inspect the gardens. Lorna's phone rang.

'Mum, Megan is so sick, she's just lying on the floor, barely breathing. Mrs Mac is here but she doesn't know whether to call the doctor or an ambulance.' Raven stuttered.

'Tell her to call an ambulance, we can't take any chances. I'll call Katrin and we'll be home in a few hours. Good girl, you did the right thing. You go outside and wait for the ambulance. Remember to lock up and you and Tammy both go with Megan to hospital. Take her list of medicines with you. We'll be there soon, love.'

They rushed back to the guest house, packed their things and were soon on the way home. Luckily they were early enough to miss the rush hour at Edinburgh and were soon pulling up in front of the cottage. Mrs Mac took a sleeping Braeden and they set off again for the hospital in Dundee. Katrin was looking after the girls and Megan was sleeping. Her face was a ghastly greenish white and the rings around her eyes were so black she looked like she'd gone a round with Mohammed Ali in his heydays.

'She's basically buggered,' the irate young doctor told them. 'Some half-wit psychiatrist decided ME was all in the mind, completely ignoring all the reams of research papers which prove it is a severe neurological condition which affects every muscle, joint and organ in the body. Unfortunately the powers-that-be were swayed by him and suggest Graded Exercise therapy for ME. It can be damaging and downright dangerous. It's like telling a diabetic they can be cured by eating sugar. Megan needs complete rest. I'm sorry there is nothing I can do except offer stronger pain relief. I can't tell you how long it will take for her to recover from this. I'll send a letter to the physio explaining that she won't be back and why. Her doctor will get my report too. I was lucky, when I did my training they brought actual ME patients in to tell us themselves what the illness was like.'

****

CHAPTER TEN

Everyone gathered for Braeden's first birthday. Megan was unable to join in so Cameron and Lorna took him through to see 'Aunty' Megan so she could wish him well and give him a little kiss. It took months before Megan was anywhere near the state she was in before. She was completely housebound and bedridden. Lorna and Cameron spent a fortune on alternative treatments and remedies. Every time they heard someone had shown some improvement they tried the treatment. Some things made a little difference to her pain and relaxation therapies helped her get a better rest but nothing made a real difference.

By the end of March she was able to shuffle through and join them for short periods. As long as she rested for a few days before and after she started going out for a cup of tea again.

As the end of April Spring decided to throw its own party. The sun beamed down with every day warmer than the last. The garden was bedecked in crocus, tulips and daffodils. throwing scent through the air. Cameron, being South African, was addicted to the barbecue or braai as he called it. They invited Mrs Mac, Kat, Amy and Duncan. Amy seemed much quieter than usual and sat at Duncan's side all night. The girls played with Braeden until his bedtime. Daddy bathed him and laid him in his cot. Lorna watched her family and friends with deep pleasure.

'Let's get married.' Megan declared.

A silence hung.

'What?' Lorna blurted.

'Damnit woman,' Cameron roared.

'Oh, did I say that out loud?' Meg asked.

'Can't you let me do one damn thing on my own. This is MY relationship, Megan, not yours.'

Lorna was shocked at how angry he was and watched nervously as he stomped into the house. He came back out moments later and sunk to one knee in front of her.

'Lorna, I love you so much, will you marry me please. Me, not Megan, or anyone else,' he drew a ring box from his pocket. 'I've known from the day I met you that you're the one. I actually had this in my pocket, planning on proposing, the day I found out Meg was ill.'

Lorna gazed in wonder at the beautiful, sparkling diamond surrounded in gold. She opened her mouth.

'Yes,' Raven, Tams, Meg, Katrin and even Mrs Mac answered before Lorna could reply.

Cameron threw his hands in the air still clutching the ring. Lorna took his hand and helped him to his feet.

'You lot stay there, don't you dare move.' She led Cameron to the bottom of the garden, away from the circle of light. Just then a full moon crept from behind a cloud and bathed them in its silvery glow.

'My liefie, I want to wake with you beside me every day, I want to close my eyes next to you for the rest of my life. Will you be my wife?'

'Cam, you've made me the happiest I've ever been in my life. Of course I'll marry you.'

Sometime later they rejoined the group amidst cheers and felicitations, Lorna displayed her ring proudly for all to see.

'We've got a wedding to plan,' Raven announced a few days later.

'And THE dress to find,' Tammy added.

'I'm not doing the white thing, been there, done that, got the Decree Absolut. Besides, I'm too old. It'll just be a Registry Office job.'

'I think I can do a bit better than a Registry Office,' declared Cameron. 'You ladies sort the dress and I'll arrange the rest. Go all out, we want it to be special. Now, I'll leave you to it, don't want to spoil the surprise.'

'Ooh, what about a designer dress? Megan can help you with that, she's got great taste,' Raven declared.

'Over my rotting carcass! I wouldn't be seen dead in designer,' Megan declared.

'What? I thought all your power suits were designer?' Lorna said.

'Nope, made them all myself. It never ceases to

amaze me how stupid women are and how they do themselves a disservice. Everyone is always banging on about the lollipop models, right?'

'Lollipop models?' Raven asked, puzzled.

'Yes, big heads and stick-like bodies. For starters, the word annoys me. "Designer". Everything is designed from the fork in your hand to the cheapest socks in the pound shop. Someone designed them. It's like when the hairdresser asks you if you want product. What the hell is "product"? Everything on earth that is produced is a product.' And Megan was back! The shadow she'd been for the last four months was receding.

'The first famous designers happened to be gay. So what do they think is attractive? They want youth, to appeal to the young and the older women all want to feel younger, so they think teenage boys. Slim, no muscles yet and straight up and down but women aren't built like that, we have breasts, waists and bums. So they go for the very skinny girls. The fashion magazines claim they have to go along with it because the designers only send size zero clothes therefore they have to find size zero models. The designers huff and say their clothes only look good on skinny women. Stupid women with more money than sense go and buy them.'

'But aren't they the best clothes?' Raven asked.

'No, they're not even the best quality, all you are paying for is the designer's name. Think about it, the designer himself has said his clothes don't look good on normal women so why would you buy them? If women stopped buying the fashion magazines the publishers would soon be demanding normal sized clothes for their models. If women stopped buying the clothes the designers would soon start designing clothes for normal women. And why are all models six foot tall? How many women do you know who are that tall? The average height of women in Britain is five foot four! Anyway, enough ranting, I'm making it.'

'Making what?' Lorna asked.

'Your wedding dress.'

'But you can't, you're too ill.'

'I've got two very capable apprentice seamstresses here. It's about time they learned to sew. And I can show them how to copy designer clothes at a thousand percent cheaper. So any ideas of what you want?'

'I'd thought a simple kind of dress, long, not white and with something over it.'

Megan grabbed a pen and envelope and started

drawing.

'Not white…hhhm… how about your favourite colours, the dress in duck egg with a teal coat in a very light, floaty fabric with a cowl hood and a hint of a train, like this?'

'It's perfect, are you sure you can make this?'

'Yep, with the girl's help.'

The wedding was set for September. Megan browsed the internet until she found the exact fabric and trimmings she wanted. They had plenty of time so she could work as she felt able. Her living room soon became a bridal workshop. The girls had a crash course in using a sewing machine, cutting out patterns and stitching beads onto fabric.

Cameron was being very secretive about the venue. Lorna was delighted to hear that her cousin, Derek, was moving back to Scotland just in time for

the wedding. At least she'd have one relative there.
As expected her parents and sister couldn't afford to
attend. Besides Pearl was pregnant so they were
ecstatic awaiting the birth of their grandchild, her
mother actually said 'first' grandchild. Never mind
the fact that they already had a grandson they hadn't
even met yet. Still, Derek was her favourite cousin
and probably the only relative she really cared about.
Cameron's parents, brother and sister-in-law were
flying over. She'd 'met' them on skype but was quite
nervous about meeting them in the flesh.

Mrs Mac and Maureen turned out to be nifty with
a sewing machine pedal too so it was decided that
raven and tammy's bridesmaids' dresses would be
made too. Mrs Mac made the cutest dungarees for
Braeden. The fabric looked like suit material and had
a little bow tie on the bib. Megan made him a teal

shirt to match the bridesmaids' dresses. Gladys insisted on making the cake as her gift to them.

After many furtive phone calls and emails, Cameron admitted that he'd booked Alnwick Lodge for the wedding. He had hired a coach to take everyone down, arranged the marriage licence, a Registrar, all the legal requirements and reserved rooms for everyone.

Mother nature produced her best sunny weekend for them. The guests all piled into the coach, leaving the back seat for Megan to lie down and sleep if at all possible in the excited atmosphere. Lorna and Cameron drove down with Braeden in Katrin's car. They were flying out to Greece for a week's honeymoon entirely alone.

As soon as Raven spotted the Vintage Travelers Wagons, the intricate paintwork painstakingly restored she laid claim to one.

'Tammy and I will share one, we're glamping!' she squealed.

'You must come and see it. It's so cute,' Tammy added.

'I'm in the Silver Bath room, there's a bedroom with a small ensuite with a shower. Then there's a kind of lounge with a huge roll-top bath in the middle facing the television. There's a sofa down the side but I'm not having anyone watch me while I loll in the bubbles watching telly,' Kat declared.

Megan was ensconced in the Tack Room. It was adapted for the disabled with a sit-down shower. The door opened straight into the communal lounge and was covered in horseshoes. Apart from Megan, they all trooped from room to room as they all claimed their unique room was the best. Amy and Duncan,

Paul and his wife, and Derek all chose one of the five Travelers Wagons set in a little field next to the car park.

On Saturday morning they all had breakfast in the wonderful Stables dining room then scurried off to dress. Keith, the co-owner, not only renovated all the antique furniture but was a gifted florist too. A beautiful bouquet from Cameron sat in their room. The lounge and function room were also bedecked with beautiful flowers from the gardens. Outside the function room was a sunken rose garden which is where the actual ceremony was to be held.

Lorna felt no nerves as she walked down the staircase and through to the garden on Derek's arm. Instead her butterflies of happiness soared. Cameron looked so handsome in his suit, with Braeden in his arms.

'My girl, I had to travel six thousand miles to find you and it was worth every inch of those miles. I promise to love you, cherish you and respect you for the rest of my life.'

'Cameron, you've made me happier than I believed possible. I promise to love you and make you as happy until the end of my days.'

Rings were exchanged and they were declared man and wife. They all moved into the function room where champagne awaited them.

'Amy is very quiet, she hasn't left Duncan's side all day,' Katrin remarked.

'Have you noticed that she is the only one wearing long sleeves? Even the men have all rolled their sleeves up it's so warm. We need to keep our eyes on her when we get home. Something isn't right,' Megan replied.

The ensuing party went on until night although Megan and Braeden had long since retired to the Tack Room. Joanne and Keith had kindly put a cot in both Megan and Mrs Mac's rooms so Mrs Mac could enjoy the festivities and then collect the sleeping Braeden from Megan's room and take him to her room.

Cameron and Lorna were in the Coachman's Lodgings – the bridal suite – the most romantic room they could wish for, with a huge fur poster bed.

After breakfast Katrin drove Lorna and Cameron to Newcastle airport for their flight. She then drove Megan and Braeden home. The others reluctantly boarded the coach. Derek was staying at the cottage with strict instructions on how to look after Megan, the girls and Braeden although the ever reliable Mrs Mac was always on hovering duty.

The Aegean sea was as blue and beautiful as promised. Lorna and Cameron spent a wonderful week relaxing, enjoying the Greek cuisine and exploring the islands by boat and on foot. Nothing was rushed or hurried, stress was a foreign language. Sun-kissed and relaxed they returned home.

Quietly Lorna tiptoed into the room. Megan lay there breathing softly. Her eyes were ringed in black and her skin a sickly white/green pallor. Lorna's heart filled with love, guilt and anger. She shouldn't have left her but Derek had promised he would look after her, promised he understood her limitations. She would kill him when she got her hands on him. Megan had obviously been overdoing things badly. Her eyes flickered, then opened. A delicious smile curled her lips.

'Sex isn't nice, it's fucking fantastic,' she purred.

'MEGAN!'

THE END

Please visit my Face Book page or contact me on alewsley@outlook.com, I'd love to hear your views. The second book in the series 'Knotted Strands' is a work in progress – watch this space!

See my other books on Amazon :

A PEEK AT LIFE – a book of 10 short stories including the award winning 'First Site'.

MIKAH THE MEERKAT GETS LOST – a children's book about a meerkat and the friends he makes on his exciting and perilous journey to find his family after getting lost in the veldt.

33798710R00143

Printed in Poland
by Amazon Fulfillment
Poland Sp. z o.o., Wrocław